COME
PLAY WITH ME

An Erotica Collection

T0337279

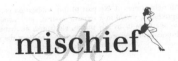

mischief

Mischief
An imprint of HarperCollins*Publishers*
77–85 Fulham Palace Road,
Hammersmith, London W6 8JB

www.mischiefbooks.com

A Paperback Original 2013

First published in Great Britain in ebook format by
HarperCollins*Publishers* 2012

A catalogue record for this book is
available from the British Library

ISBN-13: 9780007553327

Find out more about HarperCollins and the environment at
www.harpercollins.co.uk/green

CONTENTS

CONTENTS

Dancing On The Edge
Charlotte Stein

He says it in the middle of talking about something mundane – like quotas or reports or that meeting we all had last Tuesday. We're just sat here at the bar, and Johnson's gone to the toilet, and in that tiny moment that we're alone he puts his lips too close to my ear and murmurs the words: 'If you come upstairs with me once we're done here, I'll lick your clit until you come all over my face.'

They feel hot, up that close – and not just because of the content. I can feel his steamy breath, rubbing against the sensitive whorls of my ear. And I get a heated hint of his body, too, as he invades my space.

I don't know how to react. A second ago he was Michael Turner, rather quiet and sort of uninteresting colleague. Now he's a guy who propositions girls by using a word I don't think I've ever heard a man say before.

1

Not even in bed. Not even when the guy in question is actually touching me there.

Though, come to think of it, even that's rare.

But this is rarer. I feel like he's already done the deed, before I've even taken him up on the offer. My clit is suddenly huge, immense. It's eating the rest of my body in pulses and tremors, and all of them make me realise something startling.

It doesn't really take a lot to make me come. I could come like this, while staring straight forwards at my reflection in the mirror behind the bar. I can see him just to the left of me, toying with his glass of Scotch as though nothing was said – but then he glances up just a little and our eyes meet around bottles of absinthe and mint liquor, and I know.

I know I could come if he just breathed on me wrong. I'm primed like an engine; he's said the magic words and kickstarted a libido I didn't previously have. Usually I'm bored, restless, I have to work for it, push for it. I'm always on the edge and never all the way over.

But that's not the case now. Why didn't I notice those eyes of his, over morning coffee and dull chitchat? They're like neon lights, lowering on the front of a predatory sort of car. Something slick and close to the ground, ready to run me down. And his mouth ... oh, his mouth.

It's like someone pressed a blade to his face. They carved those cut-glass cheekbones, and then finished off with a slash just above his chin.

Which is all just a way of saying that he's stunningly attractive, though I'd never quite seen it before today. I guess I'd passed him by in the same manner I pass by most handsome men, sure and certain in their uninterest, only concerned with what they have to say. Maybe it'll be something good, like today.

Though usually I'm just hoping for anything at all. From anyone, ever. A word, a sign that I'm alive. A hand on my thigh as nonchalant as a back pat, just before he slides away.

Of course, I know where he's going. He's headed to that mythical upstairs – the one I can't help picturing as a bin for this bar. Beer crates on the stairs, boxes in the bare living room, naked bulbs dangling from the ceiling.

But Johnson tells me otherwise. He asks me if Michael has called it a night, and then he points to the place I was offered. 'Maybe we should head off too,' he says, while I reframe the place above with this new information in mind.

Now it's not a fuck on the stairs, amidst the rubble. There's no splinters digging into my ass, from stripped floorboards in an abandoned apartment. I think of how he seems, instead, and what the home of a man like him would be like – pristine, elegant, sharp. The way his suits are, the way his haircut is, the way he'd whispered those words in my ear.

So slick, I think.

I should be angry.

Instead, I'm walking up the stairs.

I wait until Johnson's bid me adieu outside the bar, and go through the motions of leaving as he does so – putting my gloves on, bracing myself for the cold. And then once he's gone I turn around and go back inside, to the red door he went through at the rear.

No one tries to stop me. No one says anything to me at all, so maybe he does this all the time. Invites a girl through this red rabbit hole, to a flight of stairs that couldn't be more different from the ones I'd imagined.

Everything is white, bright white, and at the top there's another door, left ajar.

Beyond, his apartment is the same. Clinical, almost, as though to take back the invitation that was so easily extended. Now I'm supposed to feel like an intruder, in the land that clean built. I'm a filthy whore who'd like her pussy licked, invading his precious space.

Though it's not this thought that makes my face heat. It's how he catches me when he emerges from some space-age kitchen. I'm in the process of fleeing, before any of this solidifies and turns into *that thing I did one time*.

'Leaving so early?' he says, and my cheeks nearly flame. I've been caught with my hand in the cookie jar, then compounded my error by vacating the scene of the crime. Now I have to be punished, I suspect, though his and my ideas of punishment differ greatly, it seems.

I think of spankings, or maybe a brutal fuck bent over his couch. He thinks of the promise he made me, and kneels down to shove my dress up over my hips. No talking. No asking. I've never been so bare before any kind of discussion has taken place.

And it gets worse. He looks up at me with this shark's grin on his gorgeous face when he sees my panties: plain cotton, humiliatingly girlish. And once he's judged them suitable, he hooks two come-hither fingers into the elastic.

Then drags them down. Slowly, slowly, as though my shivering shame and uncertainty are worth savouring. And I can tell he is savouring it, too, because he doesn't look at my newly exposed pussy, sparsely furred and already gleaming with the evidence of my arousal. He looks at my face as he inches them down, then once they're on the floor he lifts my feet to free them.

Which has the bonus of spreading my legs. Once my feet are back on the ground, they're noticeably further apart than they were before – and he's still staring, too. He holds my gaze long after he's leaned in to plant an open-mouthed kiss on my split sex, all wet and warm and too much, too much.

I don't know what to do with it. I can't watch someone watching me, as he slides his tongue between my swollen lips and licks whatever he finds there. I just can't. He isn't even tender about it, holding back until I can take it, delicately forging forward when I urge him on. He grasps great handfuls of my ass and holds me there. He mashes his face right into my spread slit, and once he's as deep as he can go he licks over my slippery hole like he's searching for a way in.

Which he finds, easily. Of course he does. He's so greedy I'm surprised he hasn't lost his way down there, so eager for more that he's forgotten the breadcrumbs to get back. It's like he's drowning inside me, and when I make a startled sound he only forces himself deeper down.

He finds my clit and really *rubs* it, in a way I didn't think was possible with that particular appendage. I thought it had to be a thumb, for it to feel like that – or maybe some sort of toy of the kind he most likely has. He's that kind now, I see.

He's the kind who forces me to stand still while he works his tongue back and forth over my clit, until I'm moaning. I actually moan, even though we don't really know each other and haven't properly spoken before now.

Our first real words to each other are cries of stunned pleasure and feral grunts of satisfaction – the former from me, the latter from him. Of course the latter's from him. I can practically see the triumph in his gleaming eyes, as though this is all some strange sex-based revenge for wrongs I didn't know I'd done to him.

He's going to give me orgasms until I'm sorry for dressing him down in that meeting one time – even though I never actually have. We acknowledged each other at the photocopier, once. We saw each other in the bar downstairs, and conspired in the awkward camaraderie of colleagues who don't really know each other.

And it all somehow led to this.

'Oh, God, I'm coming,' I say, because I *have* to. It's so shocking that voicing it is a requirement, not an option. My legs are trembling, trembling, trembling and it's kind of like he's twisting something, lowdown in my gut. And then he takes my so-swollen clit between his teeth and that's it.

I make a noise like an animal dying. I grunt the way he did, five seconds ago – guttural and unfettered, full of a kind of satisfaction I've never felt before. This is what going over the edge easily feels like. This is what pleasure is.

Something that makes you sob, even though you don't want to.

Though it seems that he isn't satisfied with this. I've not given enough. I'm not the kind of mess he was hoping for. He wants to reduce me to rubble, I realise – which of course only gives credibility to that whole revenge-based idea.

But the thing is ... it doesn't feel like revenge, when he carries on making these wet, nearly unbearable circles around my clit. It feels like he's simultaneously bringing me down from the most gut-punching orgasm of my life and winding me back up into another.

It's almost good. It's almost not. It's just right on that glancing edge, perfect and blissful and nearly too much.

Seriously – where has this genius been my whole life? Why have I settled for less, when I could have had this? I mean, for God's sake – *I nodded my head at him, over the copy machine*. Which now seems like a crime punishable only by death.

From incredible orgasms.

'Stop,' I tell him. 'Stop.'

But of course he doesn't. He's on a mission, now, to make me collapse – and I know it is a mission. I can feel his fingers really digging into my ass, to keep me where I am. And when I manage to wriggle my hips he stays with me. He keeps his tongue on my clit, pressing now in this rhythmic, unsettling way that sets my nerves jangling.

It's not going to be long, I know. I can feel a different sort of orgasm building at that point of connection, so intense it's like burning. I'm not sure I'm going to be able to take it, but when it finally starts to break he keeps me rooted to him – like some unsteady tree that's somehow grown right out of his face.

I'm more connected to him, I realise, than to my last three boyfriends. There's nothing between us. No whisper of material, no veil of propriety or personal space. He's right up against me, right there with me, and, once he's done, that feeling doesn't go. He stands and steps back, but I can still see me all over his face.

And I can feel that hunger for me burning right out of him, too raw and real. This is what sex is, I think, but of course I can't actually say. It would seem like the kid who wasn't paying attention in class suddenly raising their hand to tell everyone that maths is about numbers.

It seems obvious, now. But I've been in the slow sexual group for far too long to actually say so. Instead I let him kiss me with his glossy mouth, stunned by the taste of myself but unable to say that, too. Other girls ... they've probably tasted themselves a million times. They've kissed like this: open-mouthed and ravenous, the rhythm of it so much like sex that I have to stop and check we're not actually doing it.

And they probably have men turn them around all the time, to bend them over things.

'Put your hands on the table,' he says, and, God help me, I do, I do. I can hear him unbuckling and unzipping, and even that doesn't make me hesitate. I just want to feel him unleash some of that hunger, in something other than my direction.

I want to see what it's like when it's turned around on him. Will he moan the way I did, grunt the way I did – will he pull me back onto his cock in a desperate sort of way? I don't know, I don't know, and that's the kicker.

I'm fumbling blind through a forest of him, unearthing

each delight along the way. Never sure if it's going to be something thrilling or frightening, right on the edge that's now as sharp as a knife.

And then I feel him, condom-covered but still somehow dangerous and dirty and oh so good, sliding and sliding through my slit. And I hear him, too – oh, the sound he makes when I spread my legs wider in this agitated sort of way, wanting more but not sure how to say it. How do you ask for more from someone you've barely spoken to?

By rubbing yourself against him like a rutting animal, it seems.

He doesn't even have to say anything in response. He gets the message loud and clear, and rubs right back against me. I've practically mapped every inch of his cock with my tender, swollen lips by the time he finally eases his way inside, though it's different once he's there. Bigger, thicker, forcing and spreading me open in a way that makes me gasp.

'OK?' he asks, but that's all I get. That one chance to tell him I can't take it, a second before he fucks into me again. And then again, hard enough to almost sprawl me over the table. Hard enough to send a deep, heavy sensation through my belly and out of my open mouth.

I have to wonder: did he really think I was going to say no to this? Oh, God, I can't even say no to it when he jolts into me over and over, hands so tight on my hips

I can't move. I can't breathe. I'm going to come again, I know, but I can't accept it.

It's just too easy.

He makes it too easy. He moans my name, breathlessly, and pounds that gloriously thick cock into me, and right when he's on the brink, right when he's shuddering and losing himself the way I already have, I lose it too.

I draw patterns in the wood of his table with my fingernails. I shout the name I'm only partially sure is the right one, and strain to get more of what he's giving – this intense, pulsing sensation, so unrelenting it's almost like pain. It makes me want to struggle against it, as much as it makes me want more.

And then it's over, and the choice is made.

'Again,' I tell him. 'Do it again.'

But he just laughs into my back – against the material I've soaked through, while surviving this ordeal – and asks me if I'm trying to kill him. 'I knew you'd be the death of me, you dirty little minx,' he says, though none of it's unkind. The laughing, the comment that suggests he knows me better than I know him … it's not cruel.

It's more familiar than anything else. This is the part where we're supposed to relax and enjoy each other's company, maybe lie on a bed together and while away some time. Only we've done it backwards, so now we'll have to make introductions. Flirt, gently, until we're comfortable with each other.

11

And then hold hands, as we ascend the stairs.

Luckily, he's made a good start. We're holding hands now, though I'm not sure when he took hold of mine. And I don't know when he started talking, either, first in exhausted fits and starts, then a little more, as we straighten our clothes. 'You've no idea how long I've wanted to do that to you,' he says, and instead of being silent, this time, I respond with the things I'm thinking.

'I didn't know you were paying attention,' I say, while he eyes me steadily.

Of course I realise then that he's not putting his clothes back together. He's taking them off, while we do this thing in reverse.

'Really?' he asks, then does a little more than reverse things. He reframes it entirely, like piecing together a movie from someone else's point of view. 'All those heated glances over the copy machine? Asking me if I like sugar, lingering too long at my desk? What kind of person wouldn't pay attention to things like that?'

Me, apparently. I didn't pay attention. I called those things mundane and ordinary, and all along they've been anything but. They were really signs I should have read, signals I should have been able to decode. When he said, 'Would you like a drink?' he really meant: 'I'm going to talk about your clit to you in about five minutes.'

I should have known.

But out here on the edges it's always hard to see things

clear. Up is down, left is right. A dull little comment is actually an invitation; a glance in someone's direction a promise.

When I really think about it, we've probably been dating for months.

On Wednesdays We Play
Madelynne Ellis

When the hood comes off, the light from the naked bulb stings my eyes like the radiance of a thousand suns. At first, his face is merely a black spot that eclipses the glare. Around me the air smells of damp earth and concrete and things that live in the ground. Where are we? There's a familiarity about the place. Are we underground?

Cellar … ? We're in Jason's cellar, where he keeps his wine, his amp and his toys.

Why are we in the cellar?

Unable to do much else, I blink, and slowly the blurred coloured spots clear from my vision to reveal the hard planes of a face: a narrow Roman nose, and eyes the green of tinted glass. Not Jason's face, but someone far more familiar. Someone I see every day at work, and with whom I pass the time of day by the photocopier. Only now he's neither bespectacled nor business-suited, and his wavy brown hair has lost out to a buzz cut. I stare up at Saul in wonderment and confusion. His aquiline brow is rent down the middle by a tight silvered scar, but what truly grabs my focus is his mouth. Thinned by his current expression, his lips nevertheless form a perfectly plump Cupid's bow. He has the lips of a kiss-happy hooker. The rest of him, dirty great army boots, braces worn over a dusky khaki shirt, is all mean brute. The image truly suits him.

'Comfortable?' He tests his ink-stained knuckles against the ridge of my jaw, putting just enough pressure into the action to nudge my chin upwards. 'I asked you a question.'

As if I can reply with my mouth sealed with tape. Well, I suppose I could nod my head. Not that I am comfortable. I'm distinctly uncomfortable, knowing neither why I'm here nor what's to come. When I struggle, ropes bite into my wrists and ankles, the coarse fibres unmercifully irritating the bare skin. Yep, uncomfortable – just as I like it.

'Freya – t-t-t.' He clicks his tongue as if he's faintly amused by my wriggling. Certainly it will take far more than a dainty shuffle to release me. His smile stretches impossibly broad, showing off coffee-yellowed teeth, as he snatches up a clipboard and leafs through the notes there. 'What a bad girl you've been, siphoning money from the company tea account, cheating all your fellow employees of their daily brews. Shame on you.' He throws the clipboard aside and it skitters across the concrete floor. 'So, what's it been going on … shoes, this rather fetching dress?' We both glance down at the stretchy red fabric that hugs my skin, and I finally understand who left me the note and why I was asked to dress so provocatively. I'm playing the corporate thief, caught with my hand in the cookie jar. I guess it's nicely grounded in reality, since I have borrowed from the fund recently.

A trail of sweat chills the space between my breasts as Saul's fingers creep across my cheek. He rips the tape from my mouth.

'What do you want? Ouch! That hurt.'

Saul stands tall again, and slowly shakes his head. 'You know it's lucky for you that it was me who found out about your little siphoning scheme and not one of the other pen-pushers, who'd have gone straight to the management.'

'You mean they don't know?'

More sweat prickles across my shoulders as he holds my gaze, neither confirming nor denying whether he's snitched to the higher-ups. The regular management will have my arse for this. I see the word 'thief' stamped across my employment records and the dole queue looming.

'What do you want?' I repeat my earlier question, my voice softer now, as I slide into the part. Although I already suspect I know the answer. I've seen the way he ravishes me with his gaze whenever we meet. Sexual favours in exchange for his continued silence.

'You know, I've always wanted a playmate,' he says, not entirely answering. 'Someone I could use entirely for my pleasure. Someone I could be entirely selfish with.'

Suddenly, he's right up close again. The hiss of his warm breath troubles the sensitive skin of my ear, so close that I imagine the brush of his whore's lips and maybe the catch of a tooth to snag my already heightened senses. I've frigged myself to sleep at night thinking about his lips and seeing them wrapped around one of my nipples. I've even added the detail of being handcuffed and his to utterly possess. Keeping him sweet will hardly be a chore, assuming the odd blowjob is what we're proposing here and nothing more.

One strong hand settles upon my shoulder as Saul circles behind the crude wooden chair to which I'm bound. He breathes in the scent of my hair, presses a kiss to the crown of my head and then licks the sweat from the back of my neck.

'Free me, and I'll work some magic on you now.'

He laughs at that. 'I daresay you can work plenty of magic, Sugar Lips, but being at your mercy ain't the plan. I think I'll stick with calling the shots. It amuses me to see you trussed up and unable to stop my hands wandering anywhere they choose.' He folds his fingers over my right breast and squeezes hard. Lust shoots through my sex in response, making everything clench. Most guys are too gentle with my nipples; not Saul. His rough manipulation sends sharp spikes of pleasure through my breasts, so they are left tingling and steepled. Fear combines with anticipation as he works the nipple roughly between his thumb and the side of his index finger.

This isn't how I like to play the game. I like to be in control of my submission. Blowing him would have left me on my knees in a position of power. This just leaves me helpless.

How far does he intend to go? Will he hurt me? Will I enjoy it?

I tell myself that I won't lie still. I won't let him do anything I don't want him to do, but, with him positioned behind me, I can't even rock the chair enough to free myself of his hold upon my breasts. Instead, I'm forced to endure.

There's only one steep flight of steps up out of the cellar. It's an escape route, but it won't solve the issue with the money. I could claim he took it and is trying to frame me. The bosses are probably more amenable to the more typical forms of sexual persuasion. Things I can control.

Saul's lips slide along the length of my collarbone, so softly at first that I barely notice them – until he finds the pulse point and sucks. The whiff of his aftershave coupled with the musky scent ensnares my senses. I can't breathe. I can't act. Instead of picturing my flight up the age-worn stairs, I'm envisage myself on my knees, still tied, lavishing attention on his cock, as he slides it first in and out of my mouth, and then between my cupped breasts.

'Like it when it gets a bit rough, do you? Don't worry; it'll get a lot rougher yet.' I feel the pinch of his teeth. It hurts … It hurts so good that I can't stop the croon escaping. My back arches, pushing my breasts up and out, my lips open, gulping air, and seeking kisses.

'Stop.' The cry that escapes my lips makes no impact on his motion.

'I'll decide when we stop.' He delicately traces with his tongue the bruise he's left upon my neck, and leaves a wet trail of saliva up to my ear. 'I'm not ready to stop yet. I've barely begun. I'm going to fuck you, Freya. I'm going to get you all worked up and stretch your pleasure out so that you're not sure you'll ever find release.'

'You can't do this. I won't keep still for it.'

He moves fast, circles to face me again and presses our brows together. 'I can and I am. And I sincerely hope you won't lie still. I hope you're going to scratch and scream and fight. I do like a good fight. And you know the more you fight, the harder I'm going to fuck you, and the more I fuck you, the harder you're going to fight. Understand?'

Oh, I understand. But mind and body aren't entirely in

agreement over my reaction. I try for aloofness, while my body melts at the thought of his touch, and of rough sex on the bare floor. I imagine the feel of his cock thrusting inside of me, the heat of our bodies sliding together in perfect, violent harmony. I see myself out of control.

Damn, his knots are good.

My attempt to work a hand free prompts a snigger from Saul. He holds me still.

'Shall we start? Shall we see what goodies are on offer?' He meets my gaze, green eyes twinkling. Then he pulls a knife from a sheath on his belt.

My heart-rate soars, my body goes into nuclear melt-down as he slices open the front of my dress. The stretchy fabric gapes, revealing the milky tones of my skin, and a vibrant scarlet-and-cream bra-and-panties set. Incredible, how the appearance of one item can change the atmosphere so quickly. I've been too blasé up until now. I've relied on my instinct that Saul is a decent guy, but knife play is moving into territory that makes me squeak with fear.

'It's a shame, but it has to go.' The blade slices through the front of my bra. Then he slides the point downwards across the plane of my stomach. I don't make a sound. I hardly dare breathe as the cold steal kisses my skin.

'Saul ...' The glint in his eyes is impossible to decipher. Is it arousal, or just sadistic pleasure?

'There's no need to get jumpy now.'

No need? I tug at the bonds again, but there's no give. There's no running away from this.

The pounding thump of blood in my ears almost drowns out his whisper: 'Careful, now. We don't want you to get hurt.' Deliberately, he nicks me with the tip of the blade, so that a single ruby bead is wept onto the curve of my belly. I stare at it in speechless alarm, while he neatly slices the sides of my knickers so that I'm rudely exposed.

Saul shoves my knees apart, and inserts one of his between them to prevent me closing them again. It makes the ropes around my ankles pinch, but my attention is drawn away from the discomfort as he curls his hand over my bush. One large finger prods its way between the lips of my sex and jabs at my clit.

Dear God!

His finger slides smoothly, as if it's coated with oil, but it's not oil that lubricates his touch but pooled moisture drawn from my body. I'm on edge. The pungent scent of my arousal rises in the air between us. Hell, I think I'm going to come just from his touch, I'm wound so tight. My clit aches, it stands proud and my pitiful attempts to recoil from the infuriatingly sweet stimulus don't change things one bit.

'No.'

'No?' His fingers don't cease their motion. 'But your body is saying otherwise. I think you want me to continue.

In fact, I think you want me to draw this out, hold you right on the edge until you're almost crazy with it. But should I let you come?' His lips quirk into a malevolent smile. 'I think you'll have to earn that release, don't you?'

I ought to demand that we play safe, but we're beyond the realm of agreed safe words and fuck-buddy antics. Instead, I'm ensnared in a world made entirely to his liking.

'Cry out if you like,' he says, knowing that I'll hate to make a sound. I bite my lips, but the sparks that kindle in my clit and thread out across my body make me want to scream and thrash about in pleasure. His fingers torment me with the promise of climax, but never quite deliver. I'm right on the edge of a delicate sexual precipice when he pinches my clit, bringing numbness and frustration in place of release.

'Bastard!'

'Yes, yes, that's right.' He releases his fly and palms the rosy head of his cock. 'Repentance before absolution.' He draws back a little way, and slumps onto an ancient sofa. His legs stretch out before him, the tips of his mighty boots almost touching the toes of my shiny red stilettos, and his hand and wrist work.

He'll come, and I won't. I'll be forced to rouse him from a state of slumber after the fact.

'Don't do this,' I plead.

Does his gaze soften a fraction? Perhaps. Perhaps it's

just a trick of the light, or desperate wishful thinking, for when I look again there's only glassy hardness and an irritable, unfathomable, sense of restraint.

'My hands are tied. I can't do you without permission and I don't have that permission.'

'What? Permission – what permission? What are you talking about?'

'I'm not the boss, Freya, just the understudy.'

Of course, I should have realised. This is Jason's house. He has to be aware of our presence. He's probably around somewhere. That somewhere is far closer than I thought. I catch the faint trace of his aftershave and realise that he's here with us in the room, watching. Saul's gaze slips over my shoulder to the inky shadows beyond. With a series of ungainly jerks I somehow manage to shuffle the chair around.

Jason is slouched in a chair beside a tripod-mounted video camera. His long legs are hooked over the arm of the chair.

'I can't let Saul fuck you. That wouldn't suit his punishment at all.' Jason's voice is silky but there's a purr of strength behind his soothing tone, which for some reason further sets me off balance.

'Why is he being punished?'

Jason's smile lights his whole face. 'You might not be able to keep your fingers out of the cookie jar, Ms Thief, but Saul here has a rather more severe habit. He thinks it's OK to fuck on company time. He seems to see my desk as the perfect trysting spot. How many secretaries have you shagged there this month?'

'One or two.' Saul mutters the reply. From the slick sounds I can hear, he's still working his cock.

'More than one or two.' Jason meaningfully rests a hand upon the camera. 'I think I have at least six on tape.'

'If you do, it's your fault.'

'How is it my fault?' The boss flicks aside his hair, which is long and dark but streaked with strands of silver.

'You wouldn't let me have her.' Saul jabs a finger in my direction.

That impossibly bright smile of Jason's further widens. 'Oh, yeah,' he says as if that detail had somehow slipped his thoughts. 'Couldn't have you enjoying yourself too much.'

For a moment we do nothing but stare at one another. I want to laugh at the ridiculousness of the situation. Instead I wait, but Jason seems content to leave us all hanging.

'Why?' I eventually ask. 'Why wasn't he allowed to have me?'

'Ah ... Why don't you tell her?' Jason says.

The sound of Saul's wanking grows faster. 'Why don't you? Maybe I'm about to do it again.'

'Stop,' Jason snaps, and the sounds of Saul's cock-stroking immediately cease. Instead, he sits grimly on

24

the sofa, his fingers curled into the upholstery and his teeth gritted. He gives an inarticulate cry as Jason sweeps towards him and draws a single lick over the ruddy helm of his cock. 'Tell her.'

'Wanted you,' Saul hisses through clenched teeth.

'He had the temerity to call your name while we were having sex.'

I have to smile at that. What else can I do? We all have our fantasies, and sometimes they win out over our physical lovers. Frankly, the dream is often a more effective turn-on than all the subtle endearments fed to us by our partners. I look at the two men anew. I've heard the rumours, I've seen the evidence, but I still brand them both as straight in my own mind – curious, since they've no hang-ups about touching one another.

While Jason returns to the camera, I leapfrog my chair backwards to where Saul rests upon the sofa. 'Did you really?'

'I fuck you in my dreams every night.'

'Silence!' Jason swipes a lantern off the table beyond the tripod, leaving speckled dots of blood-red wax across the floor. The shattered glass crunches beneath his boots as he turns to us again. 'No consorting among prisoners.'

'So I'm a prisoner too now, am I? Are you going to tie me up?' Saul holds out his wrists.

'No. You're going to sit there and sweat while I fuck your dream lover.'

'Hey,' I protest. 'Don't I get a say in this?'

Jason shrugs off his leather coat, beneath which he's wearing black jeans. He's shirtless, his torso ripped with hard-earned muscle. His smoothness is the perfect opposite of Saul's hairy ruggedness. He cradles my chin in the V between his forefinger and thumb. 'You took without permission. I'm going to take without permission. Later, you're going to make Saul come, and you'd better make sure that it's my name he screams when he does, or we're going to be here a very long time.'

'You're insane.'

'I prefer to think of it as mildly delusional.' He presses his lips to mine, slowly building the pressure, to which I willingly yield.

'I'll cry out,' I warn him.

'Fuck, I do hope so. I hope you scream.'

'Someone will hear. You can't just take what you want.'

'Saul will hear. The camera will hear. Beyond that …' He brushes his lips against mine again. 'I don't think you'll call out. I don't even think you'll run.' He unfastens the knots that bind my wrists and ankles. On shaky legs, I stand. And he's right: even as the blood floods back to my limbs, I don't run, not even when he gives me the space to do so. I'm too intrigued, too excited by the idea of what's to come. Besides, I'm free now. I'm in control. And running into the street with my clothing ripped up and my body exposed will likely gain me a whole lot more attention than I bargained for.

'Suck him.'

Saul's gaze fixes upon me as I drop to my knees between his legs. 'This is my fantasy,' I say, and it's the absolute truth. 'Why didn't you want me to suck?'

He breathes hard through his nose. 'I was supposed to be punishing you, and it's not a punishment if you're enjoying it.'

Jason shoves me towards my target. 'Less chatting – suck!'

He can think whatever he likes, but from the moment my lips hover over the crown of Saul's cock, Jason is no longer in charge. I am. Saul's every breath hangs upon my actions. I dab at him with the tip of my tongue, barely touching the skin, which is berry-red and drawn so tight it seems to have outgrown its collar. He whimpers when I cup him and add the stimulus of my thumb to the mix. Still, I make him wait, just as he intended to make me await my release. I think the only reason Jason let's me get away with the delay is that he's as enraptured by the spell I've woven between myself and Saul with two tiny touches as we both are.

'Please ... touch me, Freya.' Saul's large hands form a fist within my hair. 'Please ... be kind.'

I'm not sure kind is truly in my nature. Besides, it's heady knowing I could tease this man, with his scarred and rugged profile and his army boots, until he cried.

I scratch a fingernail down his shaft. 'I don't think

kindness is what you're really after.' The cap of his cock is so smooth. I want to circle it over and over.

'Don't come,' Jason instructs Saul. 'See he doesn't,' he adds to me.

'He's a big boy, he can control himself.' Of course, just me making mention of it implies otherwise. Saul is perhaps thinking the same. His thighs are trembling as I lower my head and take him in, all the way into my throat, right down so that my nose nuzzles into the root.

'Fucking hell!' he moans. 'That's hot.'

Easy up again. Now the impressive visuals are out of the way, I let my hands do the work along with my mouth, circling the shaft, tugging at the pulsing flesh. Slow, then fast – faster, bringing him quickly to the edge, and then drawing him back again. He croaks, and draws his bottom up off the sofa as everything pulls tight.

'Not yet,' Jason warns.

I fall back upon a tortuous tease. Saul's muscles quiver. 'Can't hold it,' he moans.

'Of course you can.' He's bathed in sweat when I rise up from the next two sucks, and fluid leaks in a steady stream from the eye.

'Just hold it there,' Jason says, which I choose to interpret as an instruction to hold Saul on the precipice rather than an order to freeze. 'Let me get in on this.'

Jason doesn't unbuckle his belt. He simply releases the fly. The image he makes with his cock poking through the slash of fabric is utterly crude, and yet compelling. It grabs me at a gut level, leaving me tense and eager for the involvement he's promised. I stare at his cock, which like the rest of him is lean and long, while he draws circles upon my bottom.

Somehow, the contrast of bare cock and his closed belt make his ethereal beauty more real. He's no Lucifer exposed like this. His virility detracts from his power, because it proves that he isn't as unmoved as his expression first suggests.

He raises me onto the sofa, so that I'm on all fours with my head in Saul's lap, then shimmies up behind me and slides his cock up and down in the channel between the cheeks of my butt.

Up and down, he strokes, driving up the air of anticipation, until we're all salivating as we wait. Waiting for that moment, when the teasing stops and the real fucking begins.

'I think you've forgotten how to fight, Ms Thief.' Jason spreads my cheeks wide and pokes his glans against the entrance to my arse.

It's true, there's no resistance left in me. I might have started out a prisoner, cajoled into this, but suggesting that I'm anything less than willing now would be an out-and-out lie. 'Just do it.'

'In the arse?'

'Any place you like.' I push myself back against him,

welcoming the way my muscles protest and then relax around his shaft. I like fighting, I like being restrained, but mostly I like being filled, and Jason fills me up until I'm stretched and each jerk of his hips forces an explosive breath from my lungs. 'May I bring him off now?' I ask.

'Like hell.' He draws me upright onto my knees, my back pressed tight to his abs, while his hands rake across my chest, leaving the nipples perked up and sore from his pinches. The sting makes me long for the sensation of a warm mouth latched upon them, sucking, soothing the ache. It's building in my sex too.

Jason's other hand snakes downwards. Two fingers spear between my curls and trap my clit, squeezing it until it too is unbearably sensitised. Only then does he relent and poke those two fingers into the aching void inside me. Aroused beyond measure I grind myself against the palm of his hand. The torture continues, nipples, clit, pussy, arse – his cock still there, filling me and frustrating me. I want to come. I want more.

'You could let Saul fuck me too.'

Saul stares at me, his mouth agape, green eyes twinkling in the half-light. Yes, says his expression, even though he doesn't say a thing.

'And why would I want to do that?' Jason's hand upon my breast moves up to encompass the base of my throat. Saul's gaze is unblinking as he drinks down the vision of us, and the way our flesh quivers as it smacks together. The movements of his hands upon the sofa are slow now. Slow and steady. 'It sounds like a bit too much fun for Saul.'

'It'd be fun for us all, especially you.' I slip my arm up into Jason's hair, and pull him towards me for a kiss. 'Aren't you just a little bit curious?'

'No.'

But I can tell just from the hitch in his breathing that he is. Not only is he interested, I'd swear they've discussed this, maybe even worked out the best position.

'I want to feel his cock sliding alongside yours,' I whisper into his mouth. 'I want to feel your prick in my arse and his in my cunt. I want that tightness, that edge where the line between pleasure and pain blurs and nothing truly makes sense any more. I want you both to fuck me hard.'

'Please,' Saul adds his voice to the plea. 'You'd still be on top.'

'Yeah,' I agree. 'If you think you can keep us both in line, that is.'

The challenge works. 'Damnit!' Jason snaps. 'OK.'

Saul is up off the sofa before any of us can blink. He kneels before me, his hard cock in his hand as he guides it between my spread thighs. 'Easy now.' He finds the angle. We all hold still as he presses home. The pressure is intense, as is the feeling of fullness. I moan. I want to jerk away, but at the same time I long to prolong the intensity.

31

So close! I can barely stand to have them move. God! I don't think I've ever wanted to come so much.

The lips of my sex meet with the hilt of Saul's shaft. He holds still, deeply buried. Not so Jason, who bucks again and again, driving me forward into his lover's arms. Saul smears sloppy kisses across my face. Jason bites the unblemished side of my neck, so that I'm left with twin hickeys. If this is what stealing the tea money gets me, I may yet take up a life of crime.

I'm virtually singing as I come, unable to stop the sounds escaping my throat as the spasms grip my body and blank my mind.

Jason pulls out and spills over my bottom. Saul comes into his own hand. Then we flop back onto the sofa in an ungainly pile.

'That was intense,' Saul sighs.

Jason reaches for a bottle from the wine rack and twists off the cap. He takes a swig and passes the bottle round. 'Not bad, even if Freya is lousy at sticking to her role. What happened to being scared and wanting to be used and abused?'

'Actually, I feel pretty used and abused. I'm not sure I'll walk straight tomorrow.'

'I doubt I can walk straight now.' Saul stumbles as he searches for the tissue box. He grabs a handful and offers them round. 'Whose turn is it next week?'

'Can't be mine,' I reply.

'Yours,' Jason reluctantly admits. All the strutting bravado of minutes ago fades from his posture. He glances at Saul, distinctly nervous.

'Cool. You know what I want.'

'A night with Fearne Cotton?'

'Uh-uh! Jase, you know you're going to look gorgeous in that dog collar.'

'And what do I get to be while you two are playing naughty priests?'

'Only Jason is a priest.' Saul ruffles Jason's hair. He smiles at me. 'You get to be the sinner making a confession.'

'Ah!' I wink. 'You know, I'm liking it already. What are we using as the confession booth?'

Saul wraps his arms around Jason's back from behind and rests his chin on his lover's head. 'Actually, I was thinking we could use your wardrobe. It has those wonderful lattice-work doors.'

I get tingly looking at them and running next week's meet-up in my head. It's the same frisson I get every week as we make our plans. Sometimes I get more of a buzz from the excitement of planning than I do from the actual sex. It's not always to my taste, although tonight's been good. 'OK, you can defile my wardrobe. Consider it a date.'

'Speaking of dates,' says Jason. 'I think I have one with a bath. Dirty fuck buddies welcome.'

Sugar Lumps
Rose de Fer

He's good with horses. I can see that straightaway. The way he stands before them with natural authority, the way he strokes them with a combination of affection and firmness, the way he soothes them with his low voice when they shift skittishly and stamp their feet. Like every girl who's ever been born, I've always loved horses. But I could never get them to trust me like that. Possibly because I'm too skittish myself.

'Here,' he says, passing me a lump of sugar. 'Sapphire wants you to feed her.'

I hesitate before approaching the mare. She's a magnificent creature. All sleek lines and rippling muscle, with a chestnut coat that gleams like polished mahogany. Her huge liquid eyes watch intently as John guides my hand towards her mouth. He straightens my fingers so the sugar rests on my palm like an offering. With a snort

34

of hot breath the horse dips her head and I feel her velvety lips close over the sugar. My instinct is to pull away but he holds my hand still while she snuffles up the treat and licks my palm. Then she tosses her head and paws the ground in a flirtatious display that clearly means she wants more.

'No, that's enough for you,' John laughs. 'It's Cheyenne's turn now.'

He hands me another sugar cube and indicates the palomino who is nudging Sapphire out of the way. I reach up to stroke her tawny cheek and she gives a flick of her long blonde tail. Feeling a little more sure of myself, I draw my hand down along her sinewy neck and back up to her head. The effect is so calming I swear I can almost feel my blood pressure dropping with every second I spend touching her. I inhale her rich horsy scent and feel calmer than I have in months. She closes her eyes as I scratch her forehead and smooth her forelock out of her eyes. At last I hold up the treat and she snaps it up in a flash, no doubt to keep Sapphire from beating her to it.

Now both horses watch John expectantly, blinking their long-lashed eyes. He displays his empty hands. 'That's it, girls,' he says. 'No more.'

They nod their heads as though they understand his words before stepping lightly away from the fence. While not as fickle as cats, their affections clearly come at a price.

The horses trot back to the centre of the paddock, where they caper in a private game, kicking up their heels and running in circles. They stop to nuzzle each other before casting a look back our way. I suspect the show is just for us, a reminder of how very good they are, of how much they deserve more sugar.

'They're so beautiful,' I breathe, watching them.

'Ah, but not as beautiful as you.'

His words make me blush. I'm still not accustomed to his compliments and I don't know what to say. I scuff the ground with my boot, mimicking Sapphire's coy gesture and he laughs.

We'd met in the museum of all places. It was my first time there and he saw me gazing wistfully at a landscape of rolling green fields, punctuated by galloping horses. I must have looked as frazzled as I felt because he asked if I were trying to escape into the painting.

'Is it that obvious?' I asked with a rueful laugh.

Like a true gentleman he didn't answer that. He just gave me the smile I would come to know so well and cherish as he took me by the arm and led me to the café for a cup of tea. He encouraged me with friendly small talk and it wasn't long before I was unburdening myself to him as though I were in therapy.

Mine was the usual 'boss from hell' story. My shrill and ineffectual supervisor was the queen of mixed signals. She didn't know what she wanted or how to express it;

all she knew how to express was rage and derision when I couldn't read her mind. Nothing was ever good enough for her and after months of frustration and sleepless nights I was really starting to lose it.

My companion listened attentively and nodded with sympathetic understanding. 'People are like horses,' he said, surprising me with his analogy. 'They need clear directions from a confident authority figure and they're happiest when they know exactly what's expected of them. And they should *never* be shouted at.'

I had never thought of it that way before but his words certainly struck a chord.

'That's how *my* horses are happiest anyway,' he added and my eyes widened.

'You have horses?' I exclaimed.

He'd probably seen the same girlish reaction before, but he still seemed charmed.

'Would you like to see them?' he asked. 'You do seem like you could do with a weekend in the country.'

I surprised myself by jumping at the offer. He'd picked up on more than just my need for a holiday. I had been on my own for far too long and I was in need of male attention as much as a break from the city. Vaguely I recalled a scene from a film where a lonely woman flirted with a stranger in a museum before going back to his place for an afternoon of sex. The affair ended badly and bloodily for her in the hotel lift. But I heard no warning bells in my mind at the thought of following this man home. My hesitation lasted only a moment. John had already earned my trust and I imagined that any man who kept horses must have a kind and gentle nature.

The house he took me to was an hour's drive from the city, set back from the main road and surrounded by trees and fields. Elegant without being ostentatious, it looked like the sort of place you'd find on picture postcards advertising the tranquil English countryside. It was just what I needed. *He* was just what I needed.

'I think they like you,' he says, startling me from my reverie. 'They never show off like that just for me.'

Sapphire and Cheyenne are chasing each other like kids, stopping at intervals to rear up and wave their long legs in the air, whinnying softly.

I smile, thinking of them as new friends rather than as someone's pets. Their breath steams in the crisp autumn air and I pull my coat tighter, suddenly feeling the cold. They had even made me forget the awful weather.

'Come on,' John says, 'let's go inside by the fire where you can warm up.' He doesn't miss a thing.

I follow him gratefully into the house and just as gratefully accept a glass of red wine. A fire crackles in the hearth and as my bones begin to thaw I think of the horses.

'Do they have somewhere warm to go?' I ask.

He sits beside me, smiling indulgently at what I'm sure

is a stupid question. 'I'll show you the stable if you like. I keep it nice and toasty for them but they like to run free in the paddock until dinnertime. The cold weather makes them frisky.'

Frisky. A feeling I had imagined was long gone from my repertoire. But as I look into his soft grey eyes I find my energy returning. I sigh with contentment, imagining how it must be to live like that, safe and sheltered, fed and cared for, free to run and prance outside and nibble treats from a beloved hand. A life of no confusion, no responsibility other than to be just what you are. It sounds like heaven.

Before I know it I am in his arms, my lips pressed to his, my entire being throbbing with need. His arms encircle me and hold me tightly and I melt into his embrace. He lifts me easily and carries me from the room. I give up all control and close my eyes as he takes me up a flight of stairs and down a corridor into his bedroom. When he lays me down on the bed I open my eyes. Unusually for me, I don't feel a trace of insecurity or self-consciousness. I know without asking that he is in charge, just as he was with the horses.

He undresses me slowly and I let him, enjoying my self-imposed helplessness. It calms and reassures me in a way I never would have thought possible.

When I am quite naked he surprises me by making no move to remove his own clothes. He simply stands at the foot of the bed, his eyes roaming over every inch of my bare flesh as though assessing me. I feel his gaze as I would his touch and my body responds accordingly. My heart begins to beat a little faster, my skin burns with need and I feel myself growing wet as I anticipate surrendering completely to him. He approaches me and I start to sit up, reaching for him.

'No, no,' he says, pushing me back down. 'Just lie perfectly still. I want to look at you.'

One at a time he takes my arms and stretches them above my head. A wave of desire washes over me and for a moment I feel dizzy. Then he steps back again and the deep concentration in his face makes me feel even more naked and exposed. The position forces my back to arch, thrusts my breasts up invitingly.

At last he touches me, drawing a single finger down the length of my right arm to my throat. He pauses there and I gaze at him imploringly. My sex is pulsing hungrily. But he merely smiles as the finger continues tracing its way down between my breasts. I whimper as he neglects them completely, veering around my navel to stop at the soft mound of my sex. The finger rests there and I close my eyes, my breath hitching. All my senses are wildly stimulated. I feel the cool, polished wood of the headboard against my knuckles, the silky softness of the bedclothes beneath my legs. I smell the piney aroma of the trees outside. It's as though he's gradually awakening my body, heightening my arousal and teasing every inch of me into a state of excitement bordering on madness.

When at last I feel his hands on my thighs I gasp. It's all I can do to keep from begging him to fuck me. He gently eases my legs apart, exposing the damp cleft that aches with a need so intense it hurts. He slips one hand down my inner thigh and gives a little squeeze. The nearness of his hand is almost enough. Almost. All it would take is one touch. One swift little stroke across the pearl of my clit. But when I open my eyes I see he has no intention of ending the torment.

He is still merely studying me and I wonder just what exactly he's seeing. Or looking for.

'Aren't you –' I start to ask.

He shushes me, placing a finger softly against my lips. His only answer is another enigmatic smile as he takes my hands and pulls me up into a sitting position. Then he goes to the wardrobe and opens a drawer. I hear the jingle of a tiny chain as he takes something out and returns to the bed with it.

When he holds it up I blink in confusion. I can't be sure but it looks a little like a bridle. One made to fit a person. Things have suddenly taken an unexpectedly kinky turn. But while I'm excited by the possibility of a new and strange experience, such games are completely unknown to me. I'm way out of my depth and suddenly my lust spirals away into a vortex of anxiety. Not knowing what

41

to say or how to respond, for fear of being wrong or making a fool of myself, I simply stare at the device in silence. Seconds pass with painful awkwardness while I try to think of something to say. Anything. John eventually takes my silence for consent and moves to put it on me.

Instinctively I flinch away but he grips me firmly by the arm and eases the bridle against my face. To my surprise, I don't cry out or even speak; I simply acquiesce, trusting him completely. My surrender floods me with hot desire again and I find myself vibrating with excitement. I want to play. I want to resist and be taken. I want to be enslaved; I want to be free. I shake my head a little, offering a token show of resistance, which he easily overcomes. The leather straps are cool against my cheeks and I feel a powerful throb of heat between my legs as he fastens the buckle behind my head. I tremble.

'There's a good girl,' he says soothingly, stroking my cheek as he would a horse's.

His tone calms me at once and I am immediately reassured. A little voice at the back of my mind tells me I am completely safe, that it's OK to let go, that there's nothing to feel self-conscious about.

You're standing at the door to a fantasy, I tell myself. All you have to do is walk through it.

I do.

The rich musky smell of the leather encircling my face

inspires me and I give my head a more spirited toss, struggling just enough that he has to establish control of me again. He does so at once, firmly but gently, murmuring reassuring words to me all the while.

When I am subdued again he reaches into his pocket and I blush as he withdraws a lump of sugar and holds it out to me.

I immediately do as Sapphire and Cheyenne had done and lower my head to nibble it from his hand. He strokes my head and calls me 'good girl' again and I melt with pleasure as the sugar dissolves on my tongue. I'd had no idea there was such a submissive streak in me.

But the game is far from over. Although he has tamed me for the moment, he hasn't broken me. And where would be the challenge – and indeed the fun – for him if I didn't make him earn it? After all, he's already driven me to the brink of sexual hysteria. Now it's my turn to drive him wild.

'Come on,' he says briskly, tugging at the bridle. He wants me to get up off the bed but I lower my head stubbornly and press my hands and knees down into the mattress, refusing to move. He tugs again, a little harder, and this time I pull back, actively fighting him.

I had expected such resistance to be met with force but he surprises me again by chuckling at my behaviour as though he finds it charming.

'Caitlin,' he says, his voice low and stern and irresistibly sexy. 'Now you don't want to spend the day locked in the stable, do you?'

I'm not sure how anthropomorphic I should be, but I risk a little head shake to say no, I definitely *don't* want to be locked in the stable; I want to be put through my paces.

'Come on, then.' He gives the bridle another tug and this time I obey, getting shakily to my feet.

My legs are trembling and I stumble forward like a new foal taking its very first steps. It occurs to me that a horse should have four legs, not two, and I glance at John's face for guidance. But he seems happy with me as I am and I'm grateful for that when he clips a rope underneath my chin and leads me back down the stairs and along a long uncarpeted corridor. The polished wood chills my bare feet and I take slow careful steps at his side, trying to imitate the graceful languid gait of a horse. He notices and strokes my hair.

'Good girl,' he says. Each repetition of that phrase only makes me more eager to please.

At last we come to a door and when he opens it I gasp with surprise. It's the stable. Immediately I am overwhelmed by the rich smell of hay and I breathe deeply, relishing the sensory bombardment. He was right; it *is* nice and toasty.

But it's no ordinary stable, as I discover when he guides me into a large annex. The deep-green carpet gives the illusion of grass and scattered all across the floor are little fences and rails, the kind you see in show jumping. Although these seem to have been made for horses of very small stature. Horses about my size, in fact.

An enormous picture window dominates one wall, offering me a sweeping view of the countryside, blazing with all the vibrant colours of autumn. It almost feels as though I'm in the paddock with Sapphire and Cheyenne, gazing out at the big wide world, yearning to run wild and free through the lush meadows until it's time to return to the cosy warmth of the stable.

As I peer around the room my eyes come to rest on a steamer trunk in the corner. A little surge of heat courses through me as I try to imagine what might be in it. A saddle perhaps? I certainly hope he doesn't intend to ride me! Well, not like that anyway. I wait nervously while John opens the trunk and fishes around inside it. After a few moments he finds what he is looking for and returns to me.

At first I'm puzzled by the lavish red feather but then I understand. It's a plumed headdress, the kind you see on circus horses. I bow my head and hold very still while he fastens it to the top of my bridle. I catch my reflection in the window and the sight that greets me makes me smile.

But he isn't finished with me. Next comes a full body harness with straps and buckles that criss-cross my bare breasts and loop round my upper legs, framing my sex.

Everything is on display. I have never felt so exposed – or so aroused – in my life.

'We're nearly there,' he says, removing something from a small box inside the trunk.

When I see the length of horsehair I blink in surprise. Then I smile as I imagine him fastening it to the back of the body harness. I'm completely wrong, of course, and when I see how he intends to transform me I turn scarlet and lower my head, my heart pounding with a thrill of shame and arousal. A round rubber plug is affixed to the tail and he is opening a tube of lubricant.

I blush to the roots of my hair as he turns me around and guides my hands down onto the closed lid of the trunk. He eases my legs apart and I obey his silent command to hold still. I arch my back to lift my bottom up for him and I whimper a little as he smears me with the cold lube and positions the tail against my tight opening.

'Relax,' he says.

I take a deep breath as he gently eases the plug in, filling me the way his cock would if he were to take me like that. The thought makes my sex throb in response and for a moment my legs don't feel capable of supporting me. Then he pulls me back up and I wiggle my bottom to make my tail swish against the backs of my calves, relishing the strange sensual pleasure.

John beams at me proudly. 'Who's my good girl?' he

asks. He turns me in a circle to admire his handiwork. Then he feeds me another lump of sugar.

At last it's time for the show. John leads me by the rope to the first obstacle and I step lightly over it, earning more praise. The placement of the jumps looks completely haphazard; I have no idea where I'm supposed to go next and I have to rely on him to guide me through the pattern. It's trickier than I'd have thought. He turns me in unexpected directions, forcing me to alternate legs as I step over the rails.

My tail sweeps against my legs with every step I take and the weight of the plug inside me is an exotic and dirty little thrill. John urges me to move faster and I obey, doing my very best to make him proud, to earn his praise. It's dizzyingly erotic, the simplicity of knowing exactly what's expected of me. Knowing that all I have to do is follow his instructions and go where I am led. My heart pounds with exhilaration and I catch sight of my reflection in the window as I step over a particularly high obstacle. I can't help but admire my bound and naked body, my long legs and glossy black tail. My moment of vanity costs me, however, and I knock the top rail onto the floor. I freeze instantly, horrified out of all proportion to the mistake.

But John laughs softly and flicks the rope to get me moving again and before I know it I'm at the last hurdle, the highest of all. This time I don't step; I *leap* over it, closing my eyes for a second, imagining that I have four powerful gleaming legs instead of just two and that my beloved trainer is astride me, nudging me with his heels as we take flight together.

I land gracefully on the other side, panting and holding my head high as John showers me with praise. I nibble two lumps of sugar from his palm before I fling myself into his arms, forsaking my horsy role for that of sex-starved woman.

I greedily yank open his shirt, and buttons go flying in all directions. He laughs and soon he is as naked as I am. Well, not quite. I'm still in my harness, but it doesn't impede his access in any way. He wastes no time in bending me over the trunk again and I shudder with anticipation as he sweeps my tail to one side and presses his hardness against my sex.

Then he slides in, filling me with his delicious length. Immediately I clench around him. The presence of the plug intensifies the sensation, pushing against my inner walls and stimulating me along sensitive nerve endings I didn't even know I had. My hips grind against him, urging him deeper.

I cry out as he begins to thrust in and out. He seems to know exactly how rough I like it, how hard I need it. Just as he knew from the very first moment how I'd respond to everything else he's done to me. As his cock plunders me he reaches round with his hands to clasp my breasts. He slows his rhythm to give them more attention, pinching the nipples, rolling them between thumb and forefinger to make me gasp.

It's almost more than I can stand. My arms are trembling with the effort of bracing against the trunk, and my legs threaten to buckle with every powerful thrust of his cock. But his hands are firm upon me, kneading my breasts as he pounds me again and again.

Just when I start to think I can't possibly take any more I feel the first rising throb of his climax. At the same moment he releases my breasts and his hands move to my sex and he presses his fingers against my clit, instantly sending me over the edge along with him. My body convulses with his in waves of devastating pleasure.

When it is over I hang limp in his arms, unable to support myself any longer. John guides me down onto the carpet, where I curl into a ball against his chest. He strokes my sweat-dampened hair and kisses me.

My body is still buzzing with euphoria as I gaze in wonderment at my surroundings, hardly able to believe everything that's happened. My eyes come to rest on an object I hadn't noticed before. It's a small two-wheeled cart with a seat for one person. A pair of long poles extends out from the seat and I can't help but smile as I realise that the cart isn't wide enough for a horse to pull. But it will fit me perfectly.

You Can Have Me
Justine Elyot

I had a T-shirt printed. It said, 'You Can Have Me'.

I took it out of the package and put it on right away, not bothering with a bra. It fit tight and snug, my rounded breasts stretching the 'You', my nipples warping the fat black print. It was just a bit too short to reach to the waist of my bandeau miniskirt, so the little strip of flesh between that and my navel peeked out, asking to be touched.

The skirt was made of lycra, black and shiny, its hem skimming the high part of my thighs, below the arse it outlined so pitilessly. My exposed legs ended in espadrille wedges, ankles tied in criss-crossed cotton.

I put my hair in a ponytail, filled my handbag with condoms and walked out of the door.

The workmen were still drilling into the pavement outside. Perhaps they'd be drilling into me, inside their red-striped plastic tent, before long. But not yet. I didn't want to get that dusty that soon.

Heat crept over my skin, sunshine lighting me up as I walked towards the gym. Passers-by double-took or clicked their tongues. One – a young man – started following me.

'Is that true?' he asked, eager feet dancing around me. 'What it says on your T-shirt?'

'One hundred per cent,' I said. 'But not here. There are laws.'

'Right, right. Where then?'

I shrugged as I turned into the gym car park.

'Think of somewhere. Are you a member here?'

'Uh, no.'

'Maybe I'll catch you later then.'

Disappointed, he slunk away as I pushed open the double doors and flashed my membership card at the girl behind the desk. When I bent to sign in, I saw the beginnings of her sly smile. She twisted her head around, looking for a friend or colleague with whom to exchange significant eyebrow-raises.

I straightened up, giving her a dazzling smile.

'Enjoy your day,' she said, a tiny snort at the tail-end of the exhortation.

'Oh, I will.'

I headed straight for the men's locker room.

The wave of sweat and heat hit me in the face. The

steam from the showers, thundering away at the end of the room, misted around the five bodies in various states of undress. One by one, they stopped what they were doing and looked at me.

'Women's locker room's next door,' said one, a beef-cake wrapped in a towel.

I met his eye and licked my lips.

'I know,' I said.

He stared for a moment. From the benches, a sniff, a chuckle, a 'woah'.

'Oh yeah?' he said at length, his eyes resting on my breasts. My nipples were tight and stiff, pushing against the material of the T-shirt. 'And that little message – is it for somebody in particular?'

'Mankind in general,' I said. 'Or womankind, if she's up for it.'

'Mankind in general,' he repeated. 'Did you hear that, guys?'

The others, having left off their vigorous towelling and application of deodorant, made various noises of voracious assent.

'Come on then,' said Captain Beefcake. 'Get over here and show me just what it is I can have.'

I walked through the steam until I was inches away from him. He put a huge hand on my shoulder, stopping me. He was a big bronze brute of a man. I wanted to get on my knees before him.

His fingers curled around the lower hem of my T-shirt, lifting it up over my breasts.

'Good pair,' he approved. 'Look at these nipples, guys. Hard as little pebbles.' He pinched one and I swivelled my hips, wanting to escape the pain and yet embrace it as well. He weighed the full rounded globes in his hands, feeling them up comprehensively while his four sweaty acolytes looked on, glazed of eye, dry of mouth.

'I want to put my cock between them,' he said, unknotting his towel. 'Bend over and squeeze them together.'

I leaned forward, pushing out my arse so that the lycra stretched over its curvaceous outline, and pushed my tits together until the brute's thick erect cock lay squashed between them.

'Oh, yeah,' he said, rocking gently on his feet so that his cock slid up and down between my breasts. 'Feel your nipples for me, baby.'

I flicked at them, my thighs straining to hold my bent position.

'What's her arse like?' asked the brute.

'Fucking nice,' supplied one of the watchers. 'Good big handful.'

'What are you waiting for? Get that skirt off her and your hands on.'

Two men jumped forward and began tugging at my tight black sheath.

The brute whipped his cock out of its nestling place

and grabbed a handful of my hair.

'Suck it now,' he commanded.

I wrapped my lips around his shaft and slid them down, cupping his balls in one hand.

'Keep at those tits,' he said, slapping one of them lightly with his open palm.

I fiddled again with my nipple.

My skirt was wrenched over my buttocks, baring them. I felt it fall heavily to my ankles. Two pairs of feverish hands laid themselves on my bottom, hips and thighs. While I worked my mouth up and down, breathing in the salty, nutty scent of the brute's crotch, my bum cheeks were spread and explored by fingers of men I did not know.

'What's her cunt like? Juicy?'

I felt my labia split and the space between them stuffed with impossible amounts of fingers, all busy around my clit. A couple speared their way up inside my vagina.

'Really wet.'

'Hot.'

'Tight.'

'She wants it.'

'Well,' said the brute, with some effort now, his pelvis jerking while I gobbled at him. 'Give it her then. That's all right, isn't it, babe?'

I nodded, as far as I could with his hand yanking at my hair.

'Who's first?' The voices over my shoulder pondered the order of play.

'I dunno. But we'll need ... Jim, get us a box of the ribbed from the machine, will ya?'

'Just one?' The voice was low and amused.

'For now.'

I concentrated on all the hands, all the fingers, at different points of my body. The brute had one in my hair, one on the tit I wasn't fondling, grasping it hard. The pair of men at my rear had annexed my slit; their fingers fought each other for the best positions, on my clit and inside my vagina. They were positioned and replaced constantly, a struggle that I couldn't lose, especially when I felt the stirrings of orgasm, low in my belly.

I was being used and handled by three men at once. Thick stubby fingers thrust up inside me while rough pads moved on my clit. Brute's cock surged further and further down my throat.

'She fucking loves it,' somebody said, and I came.

So did the brute, bitter liquid spattering my tongue, bursting in my mouth.

I swallowed without thinking twice, still rotating my hips as my own orgasm receded.

My mouth was empty of cock then, and the fingers moved away from my sex as well, a triple loss that I felt quite keenly. My knees were post-orgasmic rubber, but the brute held me up with his hands on my shoulders, keeping me steady for the first penetration.

I heard the latex snapping behind me.

'Who's first?'

'Does it matter?' asked brute, his voice much lower and looser than it had been, now he had spilled his load into me. 'Everyone'll get their go. We can have her. The T-shirt has spoken.'

'Well, I beat you on the squash court,' said one of the pair. 'So I reckon that gives me first dibs.'

'Go on then,' said the other, resigned. 'I'm seriously gonna work on my backhand tomorrow.'

I tried to breathe steadily, to straighten my legs and hold them taut while I waited for the first move.

'You want her like this?' asked the brute gruffly. 'Bent over? Or against the wall? Maybe I could put her on all fours.'

'Nah, this is good. Just the right height to ...'

His hands held my hips and then I was speared, so quickly I gasped and tried to jump away, but the brute had me exactly where he wanted me and I had no choice but to take that good hard cock all the way up.

'What's it like?' asked his squash partner greedily.

'Oh, yeah, so good. So fucking good. She's so wet and she really wants it ... really milks it. You want this, don't you, babe?'

'Yes,' I answered, my eyes on the floor, on brute's bare feet, his hairy toes. My breasts swung forward with each thrust; I held on to them before it became painful, but the brute took my hands off and substituted his own. I was being held up by my tits while another man banged away at me, with slow, deliberate strokes.

'Get your legs wider,' he said jerkily and I moved my feet further apart. I could see his between them, see his shins and knees edge forwards and back, see his calf muscles straining. He was doing all the work while I just took it. And what a lot there was to take.

'Touch your pussy,' said the brute. 'Go on. Give that clit a strum. You know you want to.'

I reached down and put my fingers where those others had so recently been. My clitoris felt a little swollen and overused but I caressed it anyway, lazily, in rhythm with the energetic fucking I was taking.

He came hard, crashing into my backside with a grunt, then drew out, to be instantly replaced with his squash partner, whom I suspected had been masturbating along to the performance.

'I'll try and hold out,' he said, slightly apologetic in tone, 'but this might not be the longest ride of my life.'

I didn't care. There were two more lined up when this one was done, and my pussy felt as if it could stretch and accommodate endless cock. I was hot and sticky and deep in my fantasy, a dirty girl who couldn't get enough and would always want more.

I pressed harder on my clit, my fingertips grazing the

cock that flashed in and out of me. The second cock, or third if you counted the brute's. I wanted somebody to call me a slut. If somebody called me a slut, I would come again.

'What am I?' I prompted, licking my lips, putting my hands on the brute's as he squeezed my tits like a man possessed.

'A whore,' said the brute.

'A hole,' said the man who was fucking me.

'A slut,' said his friend.

I came, clamping my mouth on to brute's forearm and moaning into the corded muscular flesh.

My rider ejaculated into his mount at that, his hands on my thighs, his skin slippery against mine.

'She needs a sports drink,' directed the brute. 'Half time. Get her a bottle from the machine, Brett.'

The brute sat me down on the benches. I put back my head against the wall and shut my eyes. The two men who had fucked me hopped back into the shower, but I was not going to do that. I wanted their sweat, their spunk, their marks all over me. I wanted to smell of fucking, of multiple partners, of filth. That was what I'd always wanted. I wanted it in my hair, in my eyes, on my tits. I wanted the evidence of fucking everywhere on my body.

Somebody put a plastic bottle in my hand and I raised it to my lips, sucking down the horribly sweet, sticky fizz. It washed away the taste of the brute's semen, which I was not altogether happy about, but it was a nice gesture, so I didn't regret it too much.

'Spread your legs,' ordered the brute. 'Let's get a look at your pussy. See if it's still in good nick.'

I complied, still with my eyes shut and my lips fastened to the sports cap.

The brute's fingers prodded around in my well-used hole.

'She can take plenty more,' he judged. 'If she wants to. Is that what you want, slut girl?'

I nodded, my clit blooming even after its vigorous employment.

'I want her arse,' said one of the onlookers.

My pussy clenched and so did my sphincter.

'I bet she'd love that,' said the brute. 'Wouldn't you, pussycat?' He sat beside me, took the bottle from my mouth and dried my lower lip with the sweep of a big fat finger.

'Yeah,' I whispered. As my lips parted, he put his finger in my mouth and wriggled it around.

'You've had cocks up there before?' he asked softly.

I nodded.

'How many?'

It was hard to talk with his finger in my mouth but I tried.

'Lots.'

'I'll bet. Any man who wants to can pull down your

59

pants and bury his cock between your arse cheeks. Isn't that right?'

'Yeth.'

'I know. You'll bend over for anyone. What about two cocks? Have you done that?'

I nodded again.

'One in the front, one in the back?'

More nodding.

'How do you fancy that, boys?' He spoke to the onlookers. 'Give her a real good time?'

'I'm game,' said one.

'Yeah. But I'm having her arse, since that was my idea.'

'Fine.'

'OK.' The brute took his finger out of my mouth and pinched my nipples sharply. 'Seconds out ... round two. Go and sit on that man's cock, slut.'

The squash players had just emerged from their shower, towels around their waists. Grinning, they drew closer to watch the show.

A good-looking dark-haired guy sat on the bench, long legs stretched out in front of him, rubbered cock pointing to his navel. I wasted no time in kneeling on the bench, legs spread either side of him, and lowering my pussy over his cock tip. It was still in good shape, no stinging yet, though I hoped there would be some by the time I left. He reached under my infamous T-shirt for my breasts and held them while I took him all the way inside. I did it slowly, rocking down a little then back up, teasing him.

He squeezed my tits and growled.

'Get on there, slut. All the way.'

I eased my way down until I sat right on his shaft, feeling its girth stretch my walls.

'Oh, you're a big boy,' I purred. He was the biggest yet, a real meaty fill-her-up number.

'You noticed,' he said, smiling. He kissed me, but that wasn't what I was here for.

I twisted my face away from him and sank my teeth into his neck.

'Oh, God,' he groaned.

I took advantage of his ecstatic confusion to start my bump and grind, nice and slow, getting him juicy. He held on to my bum cheeks and spread them apart. I sensed his friend standing behind me and guessed I should get ready for the second half of this extravaganza.

'Got lube?' Again, the machine by the toilets did its work and my little lap dance was interrupted by the cold, slippery tip of a finger between my helpfully spread cheeks. Up and down my furrow the sensation skated, then it pressed against my tight opening, cajoling it. I was so busy with the cock inside that I just let things take their course.

I opened up to the finger, then the second, enjoying the double-skewering and the slicking of the lube.

'How's that ass?' someone asked.

'Tight,' said the owner of the fingers. 'Mm, this is going to feel so good. Ready to be ass-fucked?'

I guessed that question was directed at me.

'As I'll ever be,' I said.

He put his hands on my waist and began to push against that tiny pucker with his broad cockhead. It slipped inside with a sudden jolt, and then he glided onwards. I held my breath, waiting for the pain then exhaling through it when it came. He advanced regardless, seating himself inside my bum right up to the hilt.

'God, that's a sight,' commented one of the squash players.

'Better than porn,' agreed the other.

'How's that, slut?' asked the brute. 'What's it like to be full of two fat cocks?'

'Fucking marvellous.'

He chuckled. 'You'd take more if you could, wouldn't you?'

I nodded. 'All the cocks ... all at once.'

'Well, lads,' he said. 'Nothing more to do but fuck those holes. Give it everything you've got. She needs it.'

At first it was like sailing a choppy sea, the rhythm confusing and out of kilter, but eventually the pair of them found their stride. The man who fucked my sex held me open for the man who fucked my arse. He in his turn held my shoulders so that I didn't have too much freedom or control over how I was used. One thrust, the other held still, then they swapped. I came within seconds of this, but they weren't going to let up on me yet.

'Did you hear her come?' one of them gasped.

'She ain't seen nothing yet. She's going to come until she can't see.'

'This slut is getting it.'

'It's what she wants.'

I felt my body, wet and steaming, crushed between them, impaled on them, a thing being used. I came again and it was so strong I saw spots before my eyes.

They finished inside me, the pussy man first, the arse man a few minutes later, and let me crumple down, my passages spasming helplessly.

'Christ, that was ...' said the man behind me.

'Yeah,' his friend agreed. 'Intense.'

'Get off her now,' said the brute. 'She needs a bit of time without a cock in her.'

They drew out and I lay down full-length on the bench, not caring that its wooden slats weren't the most comfortable bedding. All that mattered was getting horizontal before my head floated away from my body.

'OK, guys, shower up and let's get out of here,' said brute, in charge as usual.

They lurched off, slapping each other's backs, panting happily.

Part of me wanted to raise my head and look the brute

in the eye, but the rest of me resisted the concept of any further form of exertion. I knew he was there, though, standing over me. His shadow darkened the dancing spangles behind my eyelids.

I let my arm dangle over the side of the bench, my knuckles grazing the floor.

I heard him shift, his feet peeling themselves from the tiles and repositioning themselves. He was near my head.

'You aren't going to tell me that was enough for you, are you?' he said. His voice was low and smoky but there was a dryness in his throat that made it rasp a little.

'For now,' I whispered.

'How many was that again? Remind me.'

'One in my mouth,' I said. 'Three in my cunt. One in my arse.'

There was movement above me. The sound of muscle in motion. I could smell him, that male scent, directly overhead. He was jerking off.

'Tell me about it, slut,' he said, his breathing laboured. 'Tell me how you feel.'

'It's hard to talk,' I said, swallowing. 'Because my mouth is dry. That sort of clicky dryness.'

'You need a drink,' he said. 'Maybe I've got one for you.'

I don't think he was talking about fizzy glucose.

'So that's your mouth. What else?'

'My clit feels swollen, really sensitive, like I couldn't bear for anyone to touch it again. And my cunt's a bit sore, tender round the opening, stretched.'

'Where it had three cocks in it earlier.'

'Yeah.'

'And what about your arse?'

'Still wide open. I can feel the burn all the way up inside. I can feel where it was. Maybe there'll be another cock up there later. It's still early.'

'Oh, yes. There's time for more cocks up that big bum, plenty of time. I hope one of them'll be mine.'

'You can have me.'

I felt the warm splash on my face, my eyelids, my brow. It dripped into my hairline, clogging me up, covering me. I wanted to keep it there until it dried on me, wear it all day, my own filthy perverted face-cream.

I lifted my hands and rubbed it in.

'Oh, God,' said the brute, subsiding beside me on the bench. 'Oh, God, I can't believe you.'

'I can't believe myself sometimes,' I said.

'You got here all right then?' he said, stroking my hair.

'Yeah, no problems.'

'Hang on, I'll get you some water. You can barely speak.'

He brought a bottle of good, cold, plain wet stuff. I emptied a bit over my face before putting it to my lips and glugging.

'I did get followed though,' I said, once I had drunk deep enough to get rid of the clicky dryness.

'Really? But you were OK?'

'Yeah. He didn't follow me in here. Didn't have a membership.'

'Maybe he's waiting for you outside.'

'Maybe.'

'And when you come out, still sore and sticky from all the sex, he'll grab you in the car park and bend you over the wall. Then he'll pull down your skirt and knickers and drive himself into you, hard, while the customers come and go, cheering him on, remembering how they've all had you themselves.'

I opened my eyes at last, tingling through my exhaustion at the thought.

'Mmm,' I said.

He reached down and ruffled my hair.

'Come on. Get in the shower. The place opens properly in ten minutes.'

My tag team was still in the showers when the brute and I picked the one at the end. They watched us as the brute pressed the button to let the water flow over our heads. My eyelids unstuck and my skin was cleansed. The brute kneaded shampoo into my scalp and shower gel over my breasts while I leant against him, legs still unsteady. He stepped aside to put the bottles back and I sank to my knees, the water splashing around and above me, blinded by the never-ending stream down my face.

The brute crouched down beside me, then he sat and manoeuvred me between his thighs, wrapping me up in his ironbound arms.

We kissed in the shower stream while the other men clicked their tongues and made 'awww' noises.

'Was that good?' one of them asked. 'Did we do right?'

'You did great,' said my brute, breaking off for a moment. 'Blinding. Next time we'll have to think of somewhere else to do it. Maybe somewhere in the open air. What do you think, Miss Slutty-knickers? Do you want a next time?'

'God, yes. And you boys are all invited.'

'Who was best?' This was the squash winner.

'It's not a competition,' I said. 'But maybe we can do one of those. Maybe an endurance test. You can take turns. Who can go the longest in me. We could have categories – blowjob first, then in my cunt, then in my arse. Who do you think would win that?'

'I can go for ages in a pussy but a blowjob finishes me in seconds.'

'I'm the other way around. Well, not seconds. Minutes maybe. I don't reckon you'd last long in her arse though. God, it's tight.'

They were still arguing about this as they wandered off, towelling themselves or picking up their sports bags.

The brute and I fell back into our kiss. While he caressed me with one hand, the other reached away from us. I tried to peek at what he was doing but he held my head firm, lips locked, face angled exactly in the wrong direction for a sly glimpse.

There was a hammering at the door and a female voice called a warning.

'Jim, we need you in five. Your first gym induction's here.'

He let me go, with a breath of regret.

I looked sideways at the tiles. In the vapour he had traced four words.

'You can have me.'

The Boys Next Door
Heather Towne

I'd only gone across the hall to see if Dane had any spare eggs for breakfast. He didn't, but he invited me inside to wait as he went down to the corner grocery to pick up eggs and a few other things he needed. I was going to go with him, but then I would've missed out on the thrill of a lifetime – my first full-bore homosexual experience.

I'd known Dane for just a couple of weeks, since he moved into the apartment next to mine in the rundown building in the university section of town. He was a tall, slim, dark-haired guy with flashing brown eyes, and a warm smile was always playing about the corners of his red mouth. He was very friendly, and I reciprocated.

That morning, he had a buddy staying over, a friend from his hometown – Brennan. I first glimpsed the guy when Dane took off and I walked down the hall of his one-bedroom, headed for the washroom. The bedroom door was half open, and I couldn't help but notice the guy sprawled out on his back on the bed, sheet down around his knees.

I stopped at the door, looking in. Brennan had short, soft, straw-blond hair, a deep, golden, all-over tan, a boyish, almost feminine physique. He was small and slender, his limbs smooth and supple, chest devoid of hair and sporting two tan, puffy, girl-like nipples. His cock hung down over his smooth-shaven balls.

I gripped the doorjamb, staring at the guy. He was sleeping, his chest slowly rising and falling, his plush lips partly open, long-lashed eyelids closed. I don't know, there was just something about the sleeping beauty – he *was* beautiful, his body a boyish work of art – that stirred something in me, something I hadn't felt for a while, something I wasn't sure I wanted to feel.

For a fully-formed twenty-year-old, I was still very unsure about my own sexuality, very insecure. I'd play-kissed with boys, sure, pretending they were my 'girl-friends' and I was the lusty male, play-pumping their clothed cocks with my cock as I faked making love to them. But that was back in my old hometown, where I'd also dated girls, and passed off as a phase my own rather heightened excitement during those male-on-male play-dates (and the stains on the front of my jeans that often resulted from them).

So, as I stared at Brennan's lovely laid-out body, I

felt a stirring in my loins, strange sensations welling up inside me that I was compelled to explore further. I slipped inside the silent bedroom, walked up to the guy.

His cock seemed to swell before my staring eyes, definitely flip to the side off his balls and lengthen. His lips moved, his eyelids squeezing tighter, and he moaned. Maybe he was having a wet dream. He was a living dream to me, right before me, my own balls tingling, my cock surging with blood and stiffening in my jeans whether I liked it or not.

I liked it.

I sat down on the edge of the bed, alongside Brennan's narrow waist, slowly, carefully, quietly, holding my breath. The bed sagged but didn't creak. Brennan sighed, his clean-cut cock rising upwards, sliding in an arc up his groin as it swelled even larger. His nipples seemed to stiffen and thicken right along.

I swallowed, hard. I'd never been so close to a naked man before, a breathtakingly beautiful naked man. My breathing was ragged, my face flushed, my cock a tangled, throbbing bulge in my jeans. Brennan whimpered, and I bit my lip and reached out a finger and touched his left nipple.

The puffy pec-cap stiffened under my fingertip. Brennan's cock surged another inch longer, stretching up onto his stomach now. I was overwhelmed with curiosity, with something even more powerful. I softly traced my fingertip around Brennan's nipple, revelling in the puffy, pebbled feel of the succulent nub.

His eyes were still shut tight, his breathing regular. My trembling finger slipped off his nipple and slid down his shallow chest, his concave stomach. His skin was smooth as silk, completely unblemished. My finger bumped up against the mushroomed hood of his cock.

He stirred slightly, rolling his blond head on the pillow, his pretty face peaceful. I'd never touched another man's cock before, not skin-on-skin, anyway. I touched Brennan's cock, tracing my fingertip around the curved, meaty outline of his cap.

Maybe I shouldn't have done it. Maybe it was tantamount to sexual harassment, fondling another man's cock while he slept. I didn't even know for sure that the guy was gay, after all. But the way Brennan's dick responded – straightening, stiffening, swelling further – and the way I was feeling – roiling with fevered emotion – were all the encouragement I needed. I slid my four fingers under the guy's cock and closed them around it, clutching his shaft.

He throbbed in my damp hand, his cock feeling so strong and alive and wonderful. I burned with more heat, shimmering with excitement. The next step was an easy one: shifting my hand up and down, stroking Brennan's cock.

'Yes, Colin, that feels so good.'

I jumped, jerking Brennan's dick up, but not letting go.

His eyes were open, his baby-blue eyes, gazing warmly up into mine. He licked his lips with the tip of a kitten-pink tongue, luxuriantly stretching on the bed – my hand wrapped around his tremendous member.

'I knew you were watching. I hoped you'd do more. There's no need to be nervous, Colin. You can do what you like to my cock, my body. I'm all yours.'

I gasped for breath, flooding with joy. My fingers were choking his prick. I loosened them, shifted my palm up and down again, openly stroking another man's cock with his knowledge and approval. I looked down into Brennan's hooded eyes in a daze.

His cock was long and thick and smooth, more than man-sized on a boy's body. It was a stunning, stimulating contrast. I gripped his pulsating rod and flat-out fisted, pulling him up in my flying hand, almost right off the bed. He moaned and arched his body, spearing his cock into my shunting hand.

'Easy, Colin, you're going to make me come!'

His voice was soft and sensuous as the rest of him. I eased up on my tugging, then reluctantly set his impressive dick back down. 'I-I want to kiss you ... your body.'

He smiled, and I gulped and bent my head down, lightly pressed my lips against his lips. We both thrilled. His lips were soft and velvety as rose petals. I kissed them again, harder. Then again, longer. He kissed me back, lying there on the bed. I boldly shot out my tongue and traced the curved outline of his lips.

Then I kissed his neck, licked the smooth, tender skin. He murmured his approval. My head was dizzy, full of the sweet scent of the man so close, feeling his heat, the pulse of his naked body, tasting the silken texture of his skin. I dragged my lips, my tongue down his neck and onto his chest, over to a fully blossomed nipple.

'Yes, Colin!' Brennan breathed, as I twirled the tip of my tongue all around his bumpy areola.

I teased the golden bud even harder and higher with my tongue, revelling in the response I was eliciting from the man – another man – the taste and topography of his intimate protuberance. Then I curled my tongue up and licked his nipple, poured my lips over it, took it into my mouth and sucked on it.

'Mmmm!' Brennan exhaled, his chest heaving under my mouth.

I sucked hard on his rubbery nipple, pulling with my lips, my cheeks billowing, nursing with delight. Then I pulled my head back and let the bud pop out of my mouth. It shone with my spit. I bobbed my head over to his other chest-cap, sucked that into my mouth and tugged on it.

It was all so natural, so wonderful. I clutched his thin, heated pecs with my hands and pulled on his nipples with my mouth. I fed like a hungry child, denied too long.

Brennan squirmed beneath me, thrusting up his chest, his nipples filling my mouth. I knew where I had to go next. And so did Brennan.

'Kiss my cock, Colin! Suck my cock!'

A man was saying it to me. I was going to do it, for the first time.

I took a long last pull on his nipple and then let go of his chest. I looked down at his cock. It seemed to be stretching up towards me, twitching for my hand and mouth. I pressed my tongue in between Brennan's pecs and dragged it downward, over his rising and falling stomach, his cute little belly button, up against the bloated hood of his cock.

He shivered, lean muscles rippling. I picked his dick up again and squeezed the pulsing shaft, curved my tongue around his carved cap like I'd used my finger earlier. Looking up at him, boldly into the man's eyes, as I swirled my tongue around and around his cockhead, gripping his shaft.

I could hardly believe what I was doing. Still, I fully realised now just how long and how much I'd wanted to hold a man's cock, lick a man's cock, suck a man's cock – the most beautiful, powerful appendage on a man's body. And now I was doing it, ablaze with passion and devoid of any second, doubting thoughts, taking Brennan's knob into my mouth and sucking on it.

'Yes, Colin! Yes!' he groaned. 'That's the way!'

His body, his cock was mine to do with as I pleased, for his pleasure and mine. His was total surrender, trust in my lust. I pushed my head down, consuming more of his prong, sliding my lips and mouth down his shaft until the tip of his dick bumped up against the back of my throat.

I kept him locked there, feeling the erotic throb of his meat in my mouth. I had total power over the man, his cock three-quarters subsumed inside of me. His eyes stared down into mine, desperately, and I pulled my head up, dragging my mouth up his shaft, lips pulling, tongue cushioning. Until I had just his bulb between my teeth, and was caressing his slickened shaft with my hand.

I gripped the base of his dick with one hand, his shaven balls with the other, and bobbed my head, really sucking on his cock. Instinctively, I knew to keep my lips curled over my teeth, so I didn't scrape his sensitive shaft; to suck slow and long and strong, then quick and tight. I knew just how to give a man maximum pleasure with my mouth. His body trembled with feeling, his cock seizing up hard as steel as I sucked.

I squeezed his sac, fingered his balls, sucking and sucking on his cock. I couldn't get enough, wanted to eat that fleshy pole whole, bite into his beefy cap and chew on it. I was blowing a man. I needed him to blow back, I needed to taste his come spurting into my mouth as I sucked him to ultimate orgasm.

But then Brennan tapped me on the head, his body shaking, other hand gripping the bedsheet. 'There's so much more we can do!' he rasped.

I pulled my lips off his pipe, drawing salty pre-come out of his slit as I did so – my first taste of another man's come! Brennan flipped over onto his front, and I was staring at the guy's taut, mounded bottom.

I knew it was time to commit myself totally. When a man offers you his ass, and you accept, there's just no going back. So I stood up on shaky legs, pulled my T-shirt over my head and dropped it down onto the carpet. Then I popped my jeans open, peeled them off. My cock sprang out in front of me and bobbed in the heated air, free to show its unabashed man-love, just as long and hard as Brennan's. The guy had his chin pillowed on the backs of his hands and he looked around, at my naked body and obscenely jutting cock. 'Niiice,' he murmured.

I climbed fully onto the bed, straddling Brennan's slim legs, my thighs touching down on the backs of his thighs, cock thrusting out over his crack. The heated feel of his tawny skin against mine made me shudder. I sank my hands onto his buttocks for support.

He groaned. I clasped his mounds, squeezed them, kneaded them, working the lush, ultra-smooth flesh with my fingers. A man's ass is just as beautiful as a woman's, and there's usually more of it. My cock vibrated, hands plying, balls skimming the backs of the guy's legs.

'Stick your hard cock in between my cheeks and frot me!' Brennan breathed.

I knew what he meant. But I had something else in my mind first – eating his luscious ass. I slid down lower on his legs and clenched his cheeks up, dropped my head down, kissed one billowed buttock, then the other.

Brennan shivered his approval.

I kissed every silky inch of his ass. Then I stuck out my tongue and smeared it all over his cheeks, really tasting his back-skin. His buttocks rippled, gleaming with my saliva. I bit deeply into one fleshy hill.

'Oooh!' Brennan squealed, arching his rear-end up into my face.

I pulled my teeth out, leaving my brand on his ass. I bit into his other butt cheek, filling my mouth with flesh and chomping down. It only whetted my appetite.

Pulling my head back up, I pulled Brennan's cheeks apart. His pucker was small and cute and pink. It winked up at me. It was time to go really deep and dirty. I thrust my tongue in between his cheeks, up against his asshole.

'Yes!' he bleated, his buttocks spasming in my hands and against my facial cheeks.

I squirmed my wet sticker against his manhole, then licked, lapped at his smooth, shaven, tender crack. He tasted so good, responded so deliciously to my licking. I dragged my tongue up and down his crack, painting his bum cleavage with my spit. His buttocks trembled out of control.

I pulled my tongue out, keeping his cheeks pulled wide apart. Then I humped up higher, and speared my straining cock into his slickened crack, in between his glorious butt cheeks. We both groaned.

I piled his cheeks up against and over my cock, burying my member in his cleavage. He cried, 'Oh, God, Colin! Frot me! Frot me!'

I pumped my hips, pistoning my cock in the hot, wet tunnel created by his buttocks. I spasmed with joy, the sensual sensations overheating my churning dick, overwhelming my body and brain. It was wicked, wild, awesome: me frotting another man with fervour.

It ended all too suddenly, but probably just in time, when Brennan flipped over onto his back, and my glistening cock stretched out over his cock, pre-come dripping from my slit onto his hood. He smiled up at me and lifted his arms. And I filled them, collapsing down on top of the guy.

Our naked bodies burned together. Our cocks pressed, squeezed together, melding us at the groins. We kissed, our arms around one another, our spirits and forms joined. Brennan's warm, moist tongue leaped into my mouth and tangled with my tongue and we frenched with fiery passion, our hips pumping against one another, cocks erotically sliding together.

It was so intimate, intense, two men tied up in each other's arms, kissing and tonguing, pumping pricks into one another. The sensuous slide of our cocks was greased by the pre-come oozing out of our caps.

Brennan broke away from my mouth. I attacked his neck, biting again, licking and kissing. 'I-I want to suck your cock, Colin! Like you sucked mine!'

I stared down at him. He grinned and nodded, pushing me up. I was reluctant to let our rutting cocks part, but I'd never been blown before, and I wanted to try everything, experience it all with my new male lover. So I rose up and straddled Brennan's chest, my hard-on thrusting out over his face.

He pulled an arm free and gripped my dong at the base. I groaned, jerking. He pumped my cock, his hot little brown hand flying up and down my raging shaft, long fingers swirling around my hood. I grunted, quivering, thrusting out my cock in his caressing hand.

He stuck out his tongue and flicked my slit. 'Jesus!' I yelped. He wound his astonishingly long licker around and around my knob, bathing my cap in heat and moisture. I glared down at the guy licking my hood, my cock gone numb with sensation.

'Suck it! Please, suck it!' I gritted.

He grinned, pink tongue retreating and red lips breaking open. He pulled my come-dripping cap into his mouth and sealed his lips over it.

I grabbed my hair, trying to control the tremoring of my body. A man was mouthing my dick! Was sucking on my cock! Brennan inhaling more of my pipe and pulling on it with his lips.

It was all I'd ever fantasised and more. My balls seemed to swell with boiling sperm, my cock seizing up come-hard, as Brennan crawled his lips further and further down my shaft, inhaling more and more of my cock into his sweet, wanton mouth, until my hairy balls pressed into his chin and my prong was swallowed whole.

The pretty boy had a depraved, dirty mouth. I was bent down his throat, locked in a molten cauldron of emotion. His blue eyes blinked up at me, watering only slightly with the pressure of all that dick in his mouth. His cheeks ballooned and his throat bulged, my prick filling his face.

I shook over him, pulsating in his mouth and throat. He slowly drew his head back onto the pillow, my vein-popped shaft sliding out from between his lips like an engorged, gleaming snake. He captured my hood with his teeth and playfully gnawed on it, looking at me from beyond my cock. Then he sucked in more again. I pushed forward, down, again, the guy consuming my prong to the balls.

He shifted his head back and forth, sucking on my cock. I pumped my hips, fucking his face. Sweat gilded my body and dewed my face, my soul soaring. It felt so fine, so exquisite – another man sucking my cock long and tight and deep. I never wanted it to end.

But Brennan ended it, disgorging my schlong completely this time and licking at the underside of the massive, quivering member with his tongue. He lapped at my shaft, bathing the beating underside with his pink licker, swirling up and around, almost coiling his tongue right around.

I clenched my fists and shuddered, cock trembling with delight. And then I took the sexual initiative again, rising higher, sliding forward, so that my balls hung over Brennan's open mouth. I'd never been tea-bagged before (never even heard the term until a couple of months previously), but I just couldn't let the opportunity pass.

Brennan made me wait, shooting out his tongue to neatly cleave my sac in two right down the wrinkled line. He pushed my balls apart, moved his tongue up and down, scrubbing my pouch. Then he batted one testicle around with his talented, teasing tongue, then the other. More strange, stirring feelings filled my mind and body.

'Yes!' I yelped with unrestrained glee, when Brennan finally swallowed my sac, took my balls into his mouth.

His cheeks bulged, lips stretched, my cock bisecting his face overhead. I felt his tongue tickle the matted hairs on my pouch, and then I felt what I'd been longing for – the tug of his lips on my sac. He was tea-bagging me now, with vigour, sucking on my pair of balls, my entire sac.

I arched my back and groaned, the sensations as wild as I'd hoped. His lips sealed my scrotum tight and his mouth pulled with a fearsome intensity. I thought the guy might suck my balls right off.

I had to pull back, yank my nuts out of his wet-hot vacuum. The sperm was bubbling out of the pair and up my pipe, and I just couldn't let it end there, blowing a load all over Brennan's blond hair. There was still the ultimate admission of gay lust to experience.

'You want to fuck my ass, don't you, Colin?' the man murmured, reading my filthy mind. 'Stick your huge, hard cock in my little bum and fuck me, blow out your balls inside of me?'

I couldn't have said it better myself. I'd gotten a taste of his ass (literally), but I wanted to go deep as a man could go with another, burying cock up the butt and pumping.

Brennan grinned as I shakily smiled, weakly nodded. I swung my leg off of him, drawing my dripping cock and balls away from his face. He slowly rolled over, still smiling. I looked down at his bronze, mounded bottom, mesmerised.

'You'll need this,' he said twice, before I responded. He'd taken a bottle of lube out of the nightstand next to my buddy's bed and was handing it to me.

I took it from him, looked at it, looked at his little butt, my large iron-hard erection. And suddenly I wasn't sure any more. I was shaken. The whole thing seemed crazy, way beyond my reckoning, now that it was all so real. I'd never had sex before, period. Let alone penetrated a strange man's ass with my cock. What the hell was I thinking?

The lube shook in my hand, my confidence shattered.

Brennan wiggled his bum and whispered, 'Do me, Colin! Please, do me! You can't stop now!'

I couldn't stop. I loved men, lusted after them. I'd sucked this guy's cock, let him suck mine; we'd kissed and frotted and pumped together. This is what gay men did – stuck their cocks in each other's asses and fucked away to ecstasy.

I swallowed hard, sucked heated air into my lungs. Then I squirted lube onto my dick and polished it. I kneed my way down lower, straddled Brennan's beautiful buttocks, pulled his left cheek aside with one hand and squirted lube into his crack with the other.

He moaned, clutching the bedsheet with both fists. I dove two fingers into his bum cleavage, rubbed. His buttocks shimmied with feeling. My forefinger found his pucker, circled it, pressed inside.

'Ooooh!' he gulped, as I sank the tip of my forefinger into his grasping starfish.

Followed by more, and more finger, until my digit was fully buried in his asshole, and I was pumping it back and forth inside of him.

He undulated his bum, convulsed his butt muscles, so that he was sucking on my anus-pumping finger. This was what my much bigger, way more sensitive cock could expect. His chute was hot and tight and hungry, steaming pink inside.

I slid another finger inside the man, pumped with the pair, his ass humping right along. Again I was caught up in the soaring sexual moment, all doubts vaporised by the awesome sexual heat. I gritted my teeth and gripped his buttock and drove my fingers back and forth in his chute, bouncing him on the bed with the renewed force of my lust.

'I'm going to fuck you, Brennan! I'm going to stick my cock in your ass – all of it – and fuck you!'

'Do it!' he wailed into the pillow, beating the mattress with his little fists.

I sawed his anus a few seconds longer. Then I yanked my digits out. His pucker closed like a flower. I mounted his ass, gripping my cock, plunged the bulbous tip down in between the man's cheeks, squished it up against his asshole.

He jerked, his butt mounds shivering. I pushed hard, unrelenting, glaring at his gorgeous bum, so needing to violate it, pour my cock into his molten chute and ream it. My dickhead popped his ass ring and plunged into his butt tunnel.

I was inside a man! I bit my lip and pushed forward,

slowly sinking inch after throbbing inch of swollen shaft into his chute. Until my balls brushed up against his wildly quivering cheeks, and I was buried inside Brennan.

I drew a breath, amazed at what I'd done. My cock thundered inside the man, pulses of pure joy pounding up from the ass-embedded tool and suffusing my body.

'Oh God, Colin! It feels so good!' Brennan gasped, again putting into words exactly what I was feeling.

I planted my hands on either side of the guy's slender body, looming over him, the pair of us joined at the ass and cock (the absolute best way for two men to get to know one another). Then I lifted up, drawing my prick back up his chute, and lowered down, filling his ass full of dick again. I was fucking him, sliding my cock back and forth in his chute. It felt sensational! My only regret was that I'd waited this long to try it.

But there was no time for regrets. I moved faster, pumping my hips, getting a thrusting rhythm going, driving my cock to and fro in Brennan's butt. Sweat poured down off my face onto his back. Muscles clenched and strained all over my body. My cock was squeezed in a sucking hot vice.

Brennan's body rippled with his own surging feelings, his butt cheeks shivering as I thumped my thighs down against them. The bed creaked, our breathing ragged and rasping, flesh smacking together.

I torqued up the pace, on fire, my cock a length of

flaming steel in the furnace of Brennan's ass. I slammed into the guy, driving him into the bed, reaming his anus, ripping him apart. My balls beat a tattoo against his buttocks.

I couldn't be stopped. I'd fuck the boy for ever. My cock was a pile-driver that had no off-switch.

But then Brennan bleated, bucked up against me. His dewy body flat-out vibrated. He was coming, blowing out his ecstasy into the sheet under the awesome pressure of my anal-ysing.

That did it! I'd made a man come! I was going to come in his ass!

I hammered into Brennan in a frenzy, fast-fucking the guy. Then I jerked, jolted by utter ecstasy like I'd never felt it before. My entire body seized up for a moment, joy steaming up my butt-buried prick. And then I jerked again, so hard it rattled my brains, and blazed come out of my cock deep into Brennan's ass.

I came again and again and again, jumping around over my equally hard-orgasming lover, jetting into Brennan's luscious ass, filling him even fuller with my liquid lust. It seemed to go on for ever, with an intensity and volume I'd never experienced before. My first orgasm inside of a man!

Finally, I collapsed down on top of Brennan, dazed, dizzy like I'd been in a whirlwind. He tremored beneath me, squeezing the last drops of passion out of my cock in his ass, his bowels and my shaft coated. It left both of us totally drained.

I kissed his perspiration-slick neck, slowly, slowly undulating my prick in the gooey mess of his bum. He rolled over, landing me on top of him, kissing him on the lips, thanking him profusely for being there for me to finally come to terms with my sexuality – emphasis on 'come'.

That's when he said, 'I have to admit that it wasn't entirely by accident. Dane told me about you. He suspected you had leanings our way. So we kind of laid a trap for you, me lying naked on the bed while he took a powder.' The guy kissed me softly on the mouth, his blue eyes shining, cock glued to my cock. 'You see, I've been "the first one" for a lot of men. Dane included.'

I grinned, delighted at the ruse. 'Maybe Dane can be the "third one", then – in a threesome with you and me.'

I'd had a man. Now I wanted more.

They Come Bearing Gifts
Giselle Renarde

Anniversaries were so much easier before Glen lost his job.

They always had enough money back then – enough to cover the mortgage, the bills, the groceries, plus all those luxurious extras, like extravagant anniversary presents.

Now they depended on Cathy's earnings for survival. The front-desk job she'd taken out of boredom when the kids started school became the family's lifeblood. Double shifts at the hotel, and still the phone bill hadn't been paid in three months. Some days, when she came home exhausted to find her husband sprawled on the couch, she wished he would swallow his pride. Glen had been very high up in his company, so it came as a shock when he was downsized. They'd been sure he was next in line for CEO.

Now they needed money, needed it badly. Cathy's boss

at the hotel offered to take Glen on at the front desk, and she'd been delighted by the idea of working side by side with her hubby, but Glen's response? 'Why should an executive settle for thirteen-hour shifts checking in hotel guests?' Her husband had his pride, and if there was one thing she'd never take from the man, that was it.

Cathy sighed as the burden of life dug into her shoulders. Every day it seemed heavier, but she closed her eyes and breathed through the tension, imagining the night ahead.

'You don't have to buy me anything,' Glen had told her, kissing her forehead in a way that always made her feel cherished. 'Being married to you is the anniversary gift that lasts all year.'

Cathy rolled her eyes, but couldn't help smiling. 'Flatterer.'

In the end, she'd come up with an evening that would knock her husband's socks off.

'What's this?' Glen asked when Cathy summoned him to the front hall.

The kids were already off at their grandparents' house, and Cathy had informed Glen that she had something up her sleeve, but she hadn't said what. She wanted it to be a surprise.

She tossed her purse over her shoulder, picked up the bag she'd packed and handed it to Glen. 'Come on, Mister. Get in the car.'

'In the car?' Glen looked stunned. 'Where are we going? Should I change my pants?'

Cathy gave him a playful smack on the bum. 'No way! Your ass looks great in those jeans.'

Glen's eyes bugged and he swallowed hard. 'What's got into you, Cath?'

'Are you blushing, Mister?' Cathy smiled so hard her cheeks hurt. 'You are! Your cheeks are red.'

'No, they're not,' he said, turning away to put on his shoes.

'Your ears are red too.' She grabbed his earlobe and tugged it playfully.

Rather than jerking his head away, Glen bared his teeth, threatening to bite her wrist, making her giggle and pull back. Cathy couldn't remember the last time they'd laughed like this, teasing and taunting one another.

'When are you going to tell me where we're headed?' Glen asked in the car. He kept fiddling with his seatbelt – he couldn't stand not being in the driver's seat.

'I'm not telling,' Cathy teased. 'You'll see when we get there.'

Glen was quiet for a while, and then he said, 'I wish you'd let me change my pants.'

'They're fine.' Cathy smirked. 'You don't need to impress anyone but me, and I'm impressed already.'

Even without glancing at him, she could sense the smile on his lips.

When Cathy pulled up in front of the hotel, Glen whipped his head around, fixating on her. 'Is it "Take your husband to work" day?'

Cathy giggled as she opened her door and handed the keys to her buddy in valet services. 'Come on, Mister! Out you go.'

Glen seemed suitably stunned, which was just the reaction she'd hoped for.

'What's going on?' he asked as Cathy waved to her co-workers.

When her boss Jamilla trotted out from behind the front desk, Glen went white as a sheet, but Cathy didn't have time to question his reaction before Jamilla handed her the room key. 'Have a great time, you two, and happy anniversary!'

Jamilla gave Cathy a motherly hug and then waved at Glen, but he didn't react at all. He didn't say a word until they were in the elevator. 'You got us a room? I thought we said no spending on gifts this year.'

'I didn't spend any money,' she replied in mock innocence. 'And I got us more than just a room.'

She led him to their suite, slid the key card through the slot and threw open the door. 'Happy anniversary!'

Glen stepped inside, and she watched him looking around with an expression of wonder painted across his face. He jumped when he arrived at the dining table in the suite's open living area, because there, holding a bottle of wine, stood another of Cathy's co-workers.

'Cripes,' Glen gasped. 'I didn't see you.'

'Happy anniversary,' said Hector, Cathy's favourite of all the room-service guys. He poured the wine, then set the bottle on the table and lifted the silver lids off their steak dinners. 'If you need anything else, just call Jamilla and I'll bring it right up.'

'How can we afford this?' Glen stammered as Hector wheeled his cart from the room and placed the 'Do Not Disturb' sign on the door handle.

'We can't.' Cathy sat before her delicious dinner and smiled as Glen wandered into the bedroom, poking around, exploring. 'But I wanted to give you something extra-special after the tough year we've had. It took some doing, but Jamilla talked to the higher-ups on our behalf, and they're giving us this night together for free.'

Glen looked stricken. He brought his hand to his heart and stammered, 'That's so ... so ... *nice*.'

'Very generous,' Cathy agreed. 'Now come and eat your steak. It'll taste all the better because we're not paying for it!'

Everything tasted sweeter for being free, right down to the Belgian chocolate mousse cups for dessert.

Leaning back in his chair, Glen said, 'I thought I'd come up with the perfect anniversary gift, but I can't top that meal.'

A glitter of pride shot through Cathy's chest. 'Oh, the

hotel room and dinner are only half the gift. You wait in the bedroom and I'll get the rest.'

She picked up her purse and rushed to the bathroom. As she tore off her clothes, she wondered what Glen was giving her this year. He'd never been great with presents – Christmas, birthday, anniversary, anything. But she wasn't done surprising him yet, and she couldn't wait to see the look on his face when she gave him the second part of her gift.

'Holy smokes!' Glen clapped his hands when Cathy sauntered into the luxurious hotel bedroom clad only in black lingerie and patent-leather heels.

'You like?' She posed for him in the doorway, giggling at his slack-jawed expression. 'Yeah, you like.'

'You bet I like!' Glen hopped from the bed, peeled off his shirt and pushed down his jeans, taking his socks off with them.

'Hold your horses,' Cathy said with a laugh, handing him the second portion of her gift.

They both settled on the bed.

'What's this?' he asked, tearing into the envelope. When the contents fell across his lap, it drew Cathy's eye to the clear outline of his erection under those suave jockey-boxers. She wanted to reach out and grab him, but held back. Glen would decide what the night held in store.

'It's a coupon book,' Cathy explained, suddenly feeling

like this was a very silly idea. 'Like the kids used to make me for Mother's Day before they had their own money to spend. Remember? They'd write up coupons for drying the dishes or vacuuming, and I could cash them in at will. Same idea here, except they're all ...' Oh, she felt very silly about this now. 'They're all ... sexy.'

She watched Glen's face as he flipped through her little handmade booklet. What was he thinking? She couldn't tell from the look on his face: unsmiling, eyes dark. Was he angry, or was he about to rip off her panties and cash in coupon number one?

'Do you like it?' Cathy asked, her voice barely audible because she was so worried he'd say no.

And then he did. He said, 'No.' And just as Cathy's heart slid into her stomach, he followed that up with: 'I love it.'

Her heart jumped to its rightful place, thumping inside her ribcage, and she smacked her husband playfully. 'Don't do that to me, Mister! You'll give me a heart attack.'

'Not before I've cashed in all these coupons, I hope.' He wiggled his eyebrows, and she smacked him again, but her gaze kept darting down to his cock. She'd been planning this night for so long that the anticipation was dizzying.

'Which one do you want to use first?' Cathy felt naughty, and it was delicious. 'Have you decided yet?'

'Oh, I've decided.' He tore a coupon from the book. 'This one first.'

Cathy looked at the slip of paper. In her own hand-writing, the words said, 'This coupon entitles you to one blowjob.'

With a self-satisfied grin, Glen got up from the bed and threw off his underwear. 'I'm ready when you are.'

'And then some!' Cathy's heart throbbed when she caught sight of her husband's impressive erection – and her heart wasn't the only thing throbbing! She crossed her legs on the bed, putting pressure on her pulsing clit, as if her rampant arousal would burst through her panties if she didn't keep it under control.

'It's been a while,' he said, cradling his dick, tempting her with its girth.

Cathy wondered if he meant it had been a while since they'd made love, or since she'd sucked his cock. In truth, the memories were hazy. They didn't get around to it as often as they should, especially now with Cathy working double shifts. She was just so tired all the time.

'I'm sorry, Mister.' Sliding off the bed, she crawled to him on her hands and knees. 'Happy anniversary.'

Glen's cock seemed to beg for her mouth, straining and growing as she approached. When she touched the tip of her tongue to the tip of his cock, he groaned so roughly Cathy was sure she'd hurt him. She tried to back away, but Glen's hands wove through her hair, clutching it. He'd never done anything like that before, and it stunned her momentarily.

Then, right back at it. She circled her tongue around his cockhead, slathering that smooth mushroom tip with saliva. His erection jumped and she had to chase it with her mouth, gobble it up before it could escape again. Glen's fists tightened in her hair, pulling it like reins on a horse, drawing her close to his body. He'd never been so brutish and forward, and Cathy had never felt so desired.

She sucked her husband's cock, letting him move inside her mouth, slowly at first, in, in, in until his dick triggered her gag reflex and she sputtered.

'You're OK,' Glen said, easing out, though not all the way. 'You're OK, just prepare yourself, Cath.'

She steeled her mind and opened her throat. When she gazed up into his face, he was a god: fit, tan, honey hair specked with silver. He'd never looked so handsome, not even when he was younger. She met his gaze and held it as he plunged into her open throat. He wore his desire like a veil before dark eyes, the flames threatening to consume her even as she devoured him.

'God, you look good down there.' He pressed her scalp, massaging it with the pads of his fingers.

Cathy moaned around Glen's erection. He'd stopped thrusting and she took full advantage, wrapping her fist around the base of his shaft, pumping his cock harder than she'd ever dared, sucking the tip, moving her lips towards the hand shuttling up and down. She worked him with hand and mouth, gazing into his eyes, worshipping him in every way possible.

Glen's heavy balls bobbed and swung, and Cathy couldn't resist them. With her free hand she cupped the fuzzy spheres. She was gentle, at first, and still Glen hissed. Then she squeezed them, and Glen stumbled back, taking her along for the ride. She lost her grip when he went a step too far and tumbled to the creamy hotel carpet, laughing.

'God, Cath, I almost came in your mouth!' Glen leaned against the wall, panting, his erection sticking straight out like a sundial.

'So what?' Cathy shrugged. 'You're allowed.'

He shook his head, his eyes still dark with lust. 'No, I'm not done with you yet. I've still got a whole pile of coupons I want to use.'

Dragging herself onto the bed, Cathy laughed. 'You don't have to use them all today, you know.'

'Are you kidding?' Glen chuckled. 'I'm using three more right now.'

Cathy's heart pounded as Glen leaned across the bed, reaching for the booklet. He flipped through the pages, tore one out and placed it upside-down on the mattress so Cathy couldn't see. He tore out another, same thing, and another, then handed all three to her, saying, 'I hope you really want to do all this stuff.'

'Of course,' Cathy replied, though there were a few items in that coupon book she felt a little iffy about. Her hands shook as she read the first one. 'Bondage. OK, that's good. I packed the bag with some scarves and things you can use.'

Glen smirked, so sexy. 'Read the next one.'

As Glen slowly stroked his cock, Cathy read the next coupon. 'Spanking. You want to tie me up and spank me?'

A canine grin took over. 'That's not all. Keep reading.'

Flipping to the next coupon, Cathy swallowed hard. 'I ... I can't say that.'

'Sure you can.' He moved in close, tracing the wet tip of his dick against her thigh. 'You wrote it.'

'Writing and saying are two different things.' Cathy's breath caught in her throat.

Glen pressed his mouth to her ear. 'Say it, Cath.'

She closed her eyes. She wasn't reading. The words were tattooed on her mind. 'This coupon entitles you to anal sex.'

Glen moaned, and his hot breath on her ear made her weak with lust. Soon his arms were around her, fiddling with her bra, releasing her breasts. He kneaded them as he kissed her, and her body was electrified. When he pinched her nipples, she felt it in her clit, like his hands were everywhere at once. God, she wanted him. She wanted what he wanted.

'The bag,' Cathy said. 'You left it by the door. There's lube in there.'

Glen ran to fetch it and came back saying, 'We've got everything but the kitchen sink in here!'

Cathy smiled at his jubilation. Glen would remember this anniversary for the rest of his life!

'How do you want me?' she asked as he pulled a bottle of lube and a silk scarf from the bag.

'Don't worry,' he replied with a snake-like grin. 'I'll show you.'

He pulled her clear off the bed, spun her around and pushed her face-down on the mattress so she was bent ninety degrees at the hips. In one swift move, he pulled her panties down to the floor. She stepped out of them without being told and felt his hard cock tracing the crack of her ass.

'Why are you fidgeting?' he asked, his voice like dark velvet.

Oh, the sensation of his hot cock brushing her hole made her blood sizzle. 'It feels …'

Grabbing her wrists, Glen forced them to meet at the small of her back, where he secured them with the scarf. Even the gentle flow of silk against her skin couldn't ease the ache in her arms and shoulders.

'It feels what?' Glen prodded as he drizzled lube all over her ass – not just in her crack or against her hole, but across the swell of her cheeks too.

'Oh,' Cathy moaned. 'That feels goooood ...'

Without warning, Glen brought his palm down on her bum, slapping so hard she jerked forward on the bed.

'How about that, hmm?' Glen smoothed both hands over her slippery bottom. 'That feel good?'

She couldn't deny it. 'Yes, Mister. Do it again.'

Smack!

Right away, no teasing, no waiting. He spanked the other cheek, spanked it again. Clapping noises ricocheted off the walls, echoing through the room, and the sound of those spankings turned Cathy on beyond reason.

'More?' Glen asked, idly stroking her ass crack with his erection.

'Yes,' she begged. 'Please!'

He smacked her ass, and a new sensation surged through her. His hand sizzled against her skin. The aftershocks burned, and when he spanked her again she wasn't ready yet. A surprised scream shattered the quiet, and she wished she could cover her mouth with her hands, but they were bound behind her back.

'More?' he asked, his voice deep and dark.

'Yes!' she cried, though her skin prickled from the spankings he'd already given her.

'Here?' Glen spanked her left cheek, the one that was still relatively fresh. Her ass sparked, but not half as much as it did when he spanked the right cheek. 'Or here? Which is better?'

'Right,' she said, without a thought.

He spanked her again and her legs shook. Thank God she wasn't depending on them to stay upright, because they would surely fail her today. Her flesh blazed under the wrath of her husband's palm, not just hot but needling, like her ass was being stabbed by thousands of tiny pins. The pain was enormous, but so arousing she never wanted it to end.

That's why Cathy was confused when Glen asked, 'Are you ready for this?'

'For what?' She tried to turn her head, but couldn't with her wrists tied behind her back.

More lube, sprayed directly against her asshole this time. She could feel the slippery stuff sneaking inside of her even before Glen's finger touched down, tracing circles around that tight little pucker.

'Put it in,' she begged. It was only a finger. She could handle a finger.

He pressed his slick digit into her ass without a word. He went slow, but stayed firm, forcing it in little by little until he'd passed right by the snug ring of her ass. Once inside, he wriggled his finger around, making perfect circles in her asshole, stretching her wider, preparing her for cock.

'Oh God, Glen!' Her clit pulsed wildly, begging for the attention she would have paid it if her hands hadn't been tied behind her back. 'Fuck me, please.'

'Where?' he asked, and all at once his cock filled her pussy, full to bursting. 'Here?'

'Glen!' she cried, her cheek pressing hard against the soft white duvet. 'Oh my God, you feel huge!'

He growled his approval, shifting slowly inside her pussy, then picking up the pace. He took up every bit of space she had to give, thrusting while he teased her grasping asshole with his finger. She had it all, and she wanted more. A finger was only a start.

She could hardly believe it when she heard herself say the words, 'Fuck my ass, Glen.'

An animal growl soared from his throat and rumbled from his body to hers. Her ass cheeks were still baking from those harsh spankings, but it didn't hurt too terribly when he grasped one and leaned against it. When he squeezed ... well, that was a different story. Cathy bit down on the clean white duvet to keep from screaming.

'Are you sure you're ready for this?' Glen pulled his finger from her asshole and spanked her raw flesh.

'Yes!' she cried as the slap rang through the bedroom. 'Fuck my ass. Don't keep me waiting.'

'I love that you want it,' Glen said, and she couldn't get over how sexy and low-pitched his voice was today. It only went that way when he was supremely turned on. 'I'm going to come so hard in your ass.'

'Yes,' she panted, her heart thumping so hard it was all she could hear.

Maybe he spoke and maybe he didn't as his cockhead met her asshole. She gasped at the smooth warmth of his tip as he drizzled yet more lube down her crack. As the slippery stuff pooled around her asshole, Glen pushed his cock in – firm, steady, just like he'd done with his finger.

But a cock was bigger than a finger, and his mushroom tip stretched the elastic ring of her ass.

'It hurts!' she cried, straining against the pressure. 'Too much, it's too big!'

Glen didn't stop. He just kept inching forward, little by little, entering her ass with a cock that had never felt so enormous.

'So close, Cath.' Glen grasped her hips, digging his fingers into her flesh. 'Almost there.'

She couldn't do it. His cock was too big. The pressure was too vast. She couldn't … she couldn't …

'Yes!' Glen growled, giving her ass a sharp spank.

She could!

He'd made it past the tight-hugging ring of her ass, and now his cockhead was blazing forth, burying itself deeper with every thrust.

Spitting the duvet from her mouth, Cathy said, 'Yes! Keep going. Fuck me, Mister!'

'Oh, I have every intention of fucking you.' He clung to her hips, racing forward, forcing himself inside her hole. 'Your ass is so hot, Cath. I'm going to come so fast.'

'Don't come yet,' she urged, bucking back as best she

could with her hand tied behind her. 'Fuck me, Glen. Fuck my goddamn asshole!'

He bottomed out and eased back, then pushed his dick forward again, ramming her, reaming her. Cathy's ass blazed, and the pressure made her weak, but she loved it. She could do this for ever, despite the ache in her shoulders and the sweat breaking between her breasts and down the small of her back. Her legs were shaking. She was screaming, shouting, 'Oh my God, Glen. You gotta come on my ass, all down my crack.'

Glen roared like he couldn't believe she'd just said those words. 'You want me to blow my load all over your pretty little asshole?'

'Fuck, yeah!' She threw herself into the saddle of his hips, milking his cock with her ass, making him groan and feeling his arousal like shockwaves through her body. 'I want you to come now. I want it all over me.'

Pressing his palms to her sizzling ass cheeks, Glen pulled out almost as slowly as he'd entered her. The suspense made her crazy, and she tried to whip around on the bed to get a better look, but the bindings on her wrists made it too hard.

'Spill it on my hole, Mister!'

'I'll spill it all over your ass crack,' Glen said, and the moment his cockhead popped out of her hole, she could hear his strong hand flapping against his dick, getting him all the way there.

'Come,' she encouraged him. 'Spill that hot cream all over me.'

Glen moaned and the flapping sound stopping. He let out a yelp as his blazing jizz met her ass crack, right above her hole. As that sweet come drizzled downward, another blast struck her asshole straight on. Another met her ass cheek, just to the left of her crack, and yet another hit her thigh. She felt so naughty, so dirty, covered as she was her husband's come, her raw ass coated with a slippery layer of lube, the rest of her body drenched with sweat. Her heart pounded. She could hardly keep up with her racing breaths, certainly not when Glen fell across the bed beside her, smiling like the cat that got the canary.

'Wow,' he said, working at the knot in her binding with one hand. 'That was just ... wow!'

'I know,' she agreed, watching the smile on his lips dance in his eyes. 'We should do that more often.'

Smiling, panting, they held hands in bed until they could work up the strength to move under the covers.

Cathy laid her cheek on Glen's chest and let him hold her, relishing the buzz and blaze of her flesh.

'Can I give you your gift now?' Glen asked.

'I think you already did,' Cathy said with a chuckle, 'but sure.' When he didn't move, she glanced up and caught that sneaky twinkle in his eye. 'What?'

He shrugged and replied, 'Oh, nothing much. Only I talked with your boss Jamilla, and told her I'd take the front-desk job. What do you think? You and me, side by side …'

Cathy's heart just about stopped. She felt her expression slip, and worried Glen would misinterpret it. She was just so blown away. Her husband had swallowed his pride and taken a job he didn't want. Now they'd be working together. No more double shifts, no more weight of the world on her shoulders, just Cathy and Glen together for ever. She couldn't imagine a better anniversary gift.

Tears pooled in her eyes as she hugged him, whispering, 'Thank you. Oh, Glen, thank you. It's perfect.'

Semi-professional
Lux Zakari

'I have a proposition for you, cowboy.' Rei's voice floated through Ethan's cellphone and was followed by her sexy giggle.

'Yeah?' He stretched out on his worn, overstuffed couch and his cat leaped onto his stomach, where it made itself comfortable. 'What's that?'

'I need you to dust off your camera and take my picture. Let's put that photography degree of yours to use.'

'How so?' Ethan scratched the cat behind its ears and received a playful bite in response.

'I realised that since I'm obviously going to be famous some day – and it's my birthday next month – I should have someone take professional photos of me. Well, at least semi-professional photos. You work cheap, I assume.'

'Hey ...'

'I'm just teasing. You know you're my favourite.'

'Favourite what?' Ethan reached forward for his pack of cigarettes on the coffee table as the cat darted into the kitchen. 'Favourite photographer? Favourite person? Favourite heartthrob?'

'You're using your imagination. Good, I like that. I knew you'd be up to helping me with my vision.'

'And what is this vision of yours, exactly?'

'Sorry, I'm not sharing my genius ideas until you agree to this.'

'I guess since it *is* for your birthday ...'

'Yes! I knew you'd come through for me. You're the best.'

He lit a cigarette. 'Flattery will get you nowhere.'

'You're a little wrong on that one. Flattery will get me anything I damn well please – especially when you see what I'll be wearing.'

Ethan shook his head and breathed out a cloud of smoke. 'I see that it's going to be one of *those* photo shoots.'

'I can't even begin to guess what you're implying.'

'Let me put it this way. Are you expecting me to mail the photos to *Playboy* or are you going to do it yourself?'

'If anyone's sending anything anywhere, it's you mailing a letter to *Penthouse Forum*,' she said. 'Now, are you up to this challenge?'

'Of course.' He flicked the ash from his cigarette in the clamshell he used as an ashtray. 'I think I can handle it.'

Rei gave a soft laugh. 'We'll see.'

* * *

Ethan was in the process of adjusting the lighting for Rei's set when he heard her knock outside his studio, which was a small, remodelled pool house set behind the apartment he rented. He yanked open the wooden door, and Rei's arms were instantly around his neck.

'I missed you.' Her Cupid's-bow mouth formed a pout and her dark eyebrows knitted together, as if he'd been the one to move back after being in New York for the past year.

'Sure you did.' He gave her a squeeze. 'Why wouldn't you?'

Rei let out a laugh – an abrupt, playful sound he suddenly realised he'd missed. 'A fair question.' She pulled away from their embrace, her eyes sparkling like she kept the world's most exciting secret. 'So! Where do I get ready?'

He pointed to a white folding screen near one of the frosted windows that almost filled one wall. 'Over there.'

'With you in the same room?' She clucked her tongue and gave him a wink. 'How are you going to resist taking a peek?'

'I'm sure I'll manage,' he said in a mock brave voice, and she giggled as she brushed past him to step behind the folding screen with the small suitcase she'd brought. He shut and locked the pool-house door and picked up his Canon SLR. Even though digital was all the rage these days, he still enjoyed the feel of a 'real' 35-millimetre in his hands.

'I hope you didn't have to cancel some hot date in order to do this for me. I'd feel just awful.' Rei's voice lacked even a hint of contrition.

'A hot date at nine in the morning?'

'I never know with you, Ethan. Even after all these years, you're still a mystery to me. You're so secretive you could probably join the CIA.'

'How do you know I'm not already mixed up with them?'

'Exactly my point.'

Ethan shook his head – a habit that always seemed to surface when Rei was concerned. He glanced towards the corner of the pool house, where he'd assembled a vintage scallop-shaped couch that he'd bought at a thrift store and reupholstered with ruby cushions; a giant abstract painting hanging on the brick wall; and a faded Oriental rug. 'I need your opinion on the set.'

'Hold on, I'll be right out.'

He'd finished winding the film on the reel and closed the back of the camera when he heard the *click-clack* of heels on the cement floor. He glanced up briefly and immediately did a double take.

Rei wore a white bandeau bikini that looked like something straight out of a James Bond movie. A gold belly chain circled her waist, and her dark hair was piled on the top of her head in a messy bun. It was then he realised that, in all their years of being friends, he'd never before seen her in a bathing suit, let alone anything this suggestive, and thus had no training wheels to see his friend in this light. Doubt crept into his mind, and he wondered if he could handle this photo shoot after all.

She appeared to have no idea of the thoughts running through his head as she put her hands on her hips and surveyed the scene. 'This looks great. I wasn't really sure how I wanted the background to look, but this is wonderful. I really like it.'

'Good.' He wasn't sure if he could trust himself to say much more.

Rei cocked her hip from side to side, shifting her weight from one shiny shoe to the next. 'So how do you want me?'

Waves of innuendoes inundated him, and although he and Rei had had no problems trading flirty one-liners in the past, he suddenly couldn't bring himself to utter one now. 'However you want.'

'But you're the photographer. All I have to do is look hot and do what you tell me to. I'm the novice here. So go ahead and boss me around. I'll do whatever you want.'

He cleaned the lens of the camera with more focus than the act required. 'OK, go for the couch.'

She obediently dropped onto the couch with a graceful flourish and gave him a devastating smile. 'Do you want me lying down?'

He bit back another answer and shrugged. 'Just do what you feel.'

'Thanks, I think I will,' she said as he put the view-finder up to his eye. But her giggles died away, and they both fell silent as the shutter opened and closed. For the first roll of film, Rei's confident demeanour dimmed, and her poses were stiff, shy and unsure. She even looked a little embarrassed.

Part of Ethan was grateful for that; her awkwardness distracted him from how she was dressed and all his dirty thoughts. He eyed the strings of her bathing suit. Just a tug, and she'd be naked. He suddenly was all too aware of his surroundings. The strange quiet that filled the room buzzed softly in his ears, and he finally put the camera aside. 'Do you want a drink?'

Relief flickered over her face as she stood. 'Maybe two.'

He poured them both a shot of the whisky he kept in his studio, while she toyed with the dusty cassette player in the corner. 'Only you would still play tapes,' she said. 'What've we got here … Billy Squier, The Law, Air Supply. I feel like I don't know you any more.'

'They were ten cents apiece at the flea market. How could I resist?'

Her mouth curved into a wry smile. 'Yes, how could you?'

There was something unreadable about her expression as she slid *The Worst of Jefferson Airplane* into the cassette player and hit 'play' without rewinding. The second verse of 'It's No Secret' filled the room and Rei made her way towards him. She picked up her shot glass and clinked it against his, and they both tossed their heads back and downed the warm amber liquid.

Ethan kept one eye on Rei and watched as she banged her shot glass down on the table, shuddering slightly and licking her lips. He subconsciously did the same. 'Another?' he asked, and she nodded.

They took their second shot, and she overturned her glass on the rickety wooden table, grimacing. Then she reached up, pulled the elastic band out of her hair and shook her hair free around her shoulders. Ethan suddenly became aware of how near she stood and immediately poured himself a third shot.

'Take it easy, cowboy.' She nudged him in the ribs. 'We've still got more pictures to take.'

He looked at her, watching him with a mysterious little smile, and he felt a pang of both anger and affection. Why would she put him in this position? Why would she have the audacity to stand so close to him while wearing so little and have no idea of the effect she was having on him? Further irritating him was how she looked at him in a way that suggested far more than their friendship had ever been – and he didn't completely mind.

'All right.' He forced aside his complicated thoughts. 'Back to the salt mines.'

'This time tell me what to do.' She touched his elbow, sending a jolt of electricity through him. 'I'm serious. I want this to be good.'

Ethan took a deep breath at the intensity of her words. 'It will be. Don't worry.' He steered her back to the couch. 'Lie on your side. Here, use this.' He handed her a throw pillow and slid it beneath her head. 'And bring your hand here.' He took her hand and moved it up to her cheek. 'And your other arm …' He manoeuvred her left arm up and over her head so that it framed her face. 'There. Perfect.'

Her teeth tugged at her bottom lip as she bit back a smile. 'Aw. You think I'm perfect.'

His breath hitched in his chest at the smouldering look she gave him. 'Yeah, you're all right.' He ignored how warm he suddenly felt and turned his attention to positioning her legs in a brusque, businesslike fashion.

'You always were so good with doling out compliments.'

He shook his head in response and returned to his camera, forcing himself to breathe deeply, calmly. He couldn't believe how ridiculous he was acting, how he was feeling. A part of him couldn't wait until the photo shoot was over and Rei went home. He wasn't sure what the other part of him wanted.

Ethan's mood lifted, though, when Rei started posing. Her expressions were more varied and natural, and she rearranged herself and moved into new positions without his direction. He started to feel a different kind of excitement from what he'd been feeling all morning. He actually felt like the photographer he worked so hard to be, instead of an awkward teenager, half-sick with lust.

Her voice broke his creative reverie. 'Ethan.'

'Hmm?'

'How long have we been friends?'

'Since sophomore year. Twelve years, I guess.'

'And in all that time, I've never heard about you being seriously involved with anyone.'

'That's because you're on a need-to-know basis.'

'And right now I need to know.'

He peered around the camera. 'Why?'

'I'm just making conversation. You're so suspicious.'

'No, I'm being professional. That's what you wanted. And I want you to sit up for this next shot.'

Rei obeyed him, moving into a sitting position. 'Actually, all I requested was semi-professional, but fine, be a bore.' A slow, mischievous grin spread across her face. 'You don't have to take it out on me just 'cause you've never bagged a babe.'

He lowered his camera and sighed as he plucked a cigarette from the half-crushed soft pack in his flannel shirt pocket. 'I think it's time for another break.'

'If you say so. I could use a costume change.' Rei swatted him on the arm as she passed him. 'I hope you're less grumpy when I come back.' She tittered with amusement and stepped behind the folding screen.

Ethan shook his head in response and lit his cigarette, noticing how his hands trembled. He glanced towards the folding screen and watched Rei's silhouette shimmy into a different pair of panties. He stifled a groan and pressed his palms to his eyelids. What was wrong with him today?

There was a scratching noise at the door and, when Ethan answered it, the cat streaked inside and across the room, disappearing behind the folding screen, where he received a warm greeting.

'Hi, baby,' Rei cooed, and Ethan watched her bend down to scoop the cat up. 'What a little lover boy you are.' She gave him plenty of loud kisses and stepped out from behind the screen, barefoot and wearing nothing but a pair of nude hipster panties, the cat covering her breasts. Ethan hoped he didn't swallow as loud as he thought he did.

'I've decided I want some pictures with the kitty here.' She nodded to the cat in her arms, which had nestled its head beneath her chin. 'Now you have to pose us both.'

'All right.' Ethan picked up his camera, the cigarette dangling from his lip. 'Go stand by the window and hope he feels like cuddling. He's not really a snuggly cat, and if he runs away on you, you'll be pretty embarrassed.'

'You'd like that, wouldn't you?' she asked, standing in a square of sunlight that tried so hard to make its way past the filthy glass.

'Why would I want you to be embarrassed?'

'That's not what I meant and you know it.'

He ignored her, concentrating instead on taking a series of black-and-white photographs of her coddling the cat and talking softly to it. He felt another tug of affection for his friend and realised he had never wanted to be a feline so much before in his life.

'What's wrong?' she asked, catching him shaking his head once again.

'Nothing.'

Rei continued to look at him and he returned her stare. The cat squirmed in her arms. She took a step forward and opened her mouth as if to speak, but the sound of a sharp click made them both jump. The cassette had finally stopped, and a heavy silence settled over the studio.

'I'll finish changing.' She moved back behind the screen and let the cat jump free from her embrace.

'Fine.' He flipped the cassette around in the tape deck and pressed 'play', wishing he could go a few seconds back in time to find out what had been on the brink of happening.

Rei reappeared a few minutes later, wearing a strapless whalebone corset that clung to her curves like a ship-wrecked passenger would to a life raft. She also wore a pair of matching ruffled panties, open-toed heels and thigh-high stockings complete with a garter belt. It was as if she'd stepped out of one of his adolescent fantasies that still continued to haunt him.

She lounged across the couch while Ethan tried his hardest not to stare at her. He was exhausted and frustrated with trying to decipher his feelings every time he glanced in her direction. She posed herself and he went to work, taking her portrait, and attempted to count the seconds as they passed by means of distraction.

'You're awfully quiet,' she murmured after several minutes of silence.

He wiped his damp palm on the side of his faded jeans. 'I'm concentrating.'

'How hard do you have to concentrate to look through a tiny window and press a button?'

'You're right, it's easy. That's why everyone has their master's in photography.' He really was trying to concentrate, but the way she suddenly decided to drape a leg over the back of the couch was making it oddly difficult.

'I'm just pointing out that you look like you're having trouble relaxing. You need to loosen up.'

119

'And how do you propose I do that?' Despite the sarcasm in his tone, he was dying to know.

She arched an eyebrow and pressed her lips together to hide a smile.

'Can you not think about sex for a few minutes?' Incidentally, he found it a struggle to think otherwise. Another surge of frustration welled inside him.

'I didn't say anything. You're jumping to conclusions. But now that you mention it, it could help you. This is why we need to find you a girl. Tell me what you're looking for.'

'I'm not looking.'

'But if you were …'

'All right, all right.' He paused, thinking. 'I guess I want someone I have a real connection with. Someone who knows me better than I know myself.' Heat crept into his cheeks then, as if he realised he had confessed too much to the wrong person.

Rei turned over so that she lay on her stomach, the curve of her ass beneath the ruffled panties peeping out, begging for his touch. She kicked one foot up in the air behind her, her shoe dangling from the tips of her toes, and propped herself up on one elbow, her fist curled under her chin. 'Go on,' she purred.

He cleared his throat and quickly took a few more pictures. 'And I'm sort of a sucker for a girl with a nice smile.'

'Yeah, and you're a funny guy. It's a good idea to have someone attractive to look at if you're gonna be telling jokes all day.'

He laughed. 'Exactly.'

She turned on her side so that she faced him and absently traced an invisible line down her throat to the top of her corset, where she undid the small silver hooks, one by one. Ethan remained frozen, unable to do anything but watch her.

Rei arched an eyebrow. 'Let's get snapping, Ansel Adams.'

Unable to dream up a comeback, Ethan held the view-finder to his eye, but his sweating, shaking hands made it impossible to take a picture. 'We need the tripod.'

'OK,' she chirped while slowly undoing the corset.

Ethan mumbled a stream of curses and willed his feet to march to where his tripod leaned against the cement wall. Why was he behaving like this? He'd never acted or felt so awkward about one of his subjects. Part of him felt guilty; Rei was one of his closest friends. How could he even think of peeling off those panties and fucking her until the studio filled with her screams?

He took a few deep breaths and begged himself to snap out of it. 'It's just been too long,' he mumbled, but he didn't believe the lie even as it slipped past his lips.

Ethan returned to Rei, who still lounged on the couch, her corset fully undone but still covering everything except the smooth span of skin from her collarbone to her belly button. He fought off a groan. She'd saved the unveiling for him. He forced himself not to look at her as he set up the tripod.

'Ready?' she asked when he'd finished.

She had no idea. He nodded stiffly, holding his breath.

Rei peeled the sides of the corset away from her body, and his whole body numbed. He had photographed hundreds of women before in various states of undress, but none of them had been Rei. He couldn't even begin to understand his reaction to her. It was an indescribable mixture of their past, both the newness and strangeness of the situation and the now undeniable need to know how the future would unfold.

'Why are you staring me like that?' She appeared both shy and pleased, two pink spots blooming on her cheeks like little flowers.

'I don't know,' he said, though he had a variety of reasons.

'Well, quit it.' She gave him a smile as she tossed the corset on the rug. 'Set up the camera and let's get going.'

He wordlessly obeyed, joining the camera and the tripod together, and, when he glanced up again, she was tugging off her panties.

'I should've warned you.' Her blush deepened and she tossed the panties in his direction. 'Things are about to get dirty.' She rolled over onto to her side, facing him and wearing nothing but her garter belt, stockings and shoes, and drummed her fingers on the couch cushions. 'Well?'

The words tumbled out before he could think them over: 'What do you think you're doing?'

Her fingers stopped drumming. 'What do you mean?'

'I ... I don't ...' Ethan couldn't form a rational thought. He closed and rubbed his eyes as if Rei were a mirage, but when he opened them again, she was still there, and she stared at him with the most horrible, crushed expression on her face. She couldn't have looked more embarrassed if she tried, and his stomach plummeted. 'We're friends,' he said, as if by way of explanation.

'And?' Her eyes became shiny and her voice quivered. 'What is that supposed to mean?'

Ethan said nothing. He had no idea any more.

'Forget it.' Rei struggled into a sitting position and reached for her discarded corset with stiff movements. Her gaze was everywhere but on him, and his face felt as hot as his chest felt hollow. It had become painfully clear that this shoot had had nothing to do with photography. He was embarrassed to have recognised what was happening so late, and his anger faded now that he understood this morning had not just been a merciless tease. But he felt frozen to the spot, unsure of how to proceed.

His mind screamed that the friendship was at stake, then switched paths completely. Images of his time spent with Rei flashed in his brain: the flirtatious banter, the intimate conversations until the early morning, the way they trusted each other more than anyone else. He wondered if they had ever really, truthfully only been just friends.

He licked his dry lips. 'Rei, hold on.'

'I have to go.'

'Don't. I want you to stay.'

Ethan's head buzzed as he walked towards her, and her eyes widened with every step he took. He stopped in front of her and tugged the corset out of her hands before crawling into her arms and guiding her back down on the couch. Then he covered her body with his and kissed her with an intensity that felt long overdue.

Rei let out a moan as his lips nipped at hers. Her fingers laced through his hair while his hands travelled over her smooth skin, making up for lost time. Her legs circled his waist, her stockings making a *hush-hush* sound as they rubbed against his jeans. Ethan kissed a path from her neck to her shoulders to her breasts until she writhed against him, needy whimpers falling from her lips.

'Please, Ethan.' She pushed his flannel shirt off his arms, leaving him in his T-shirt and jeans. 'I'm done waiting.'

He rose on his forearms as she worked a hand between them and he suppressed a moan at the sight of her, naked and needy beneath him. She reached for his belt buckle and unzipped his jeans, freeing him. He let out a shaky breath as her hand closed around him and watched her stroke his shaft.

'Are you all right with this?' Her smoky eyes burned holes into his.

He gave her a wavering smile, his attention reserved for her hand on his cock. 'Guess.'

She shook her head with a shy grin. 'You know what I mean.'

He drew in a shaky breath and closed his eyes as he nodded. His earlier annoyance had morphed into lust and even fear at the realisation at how normal everything felt. How right.

Her eyes sparkled. 'You aren't caving into my charms just because I'm a sure thing, are you?'

Ethan brushed his lips against hers. 'A sure thing is the one thing you're not.'

Rei curled her arms around his neck, pressing her chest to his and deepening their kiss. He snaked a hand between her legs and found her already wet. She arched her back at his gentle touch and he stifled a moan. The heels of her shoes scratched against the backs of his calves as he traced a wet circle around her clit with his finger. His head clouded with pleasure as he sank a finger inside her, and her breathy moan against his ear was the most beautiful sound he'd ever heard. She rocked against his hand, and he couldn't believe that this was happening between him and his closest friend.

'I just have one more question,' she said between gasps.

'What?' He braced himself for the worst, all the while finding it difficult to concentrate on her words with her pussy clutching his fingers.

'Do you care if I keep my shoes and stockings on?'

He breathed out a laugh against her neck, relieved. 'By all means.'

Rei pressed her lips together in an effort to smother a giggle, but her eyes were shining with amusement. This was strange, new territory, but it didn't seem to matter enough to stop.

His heart hammered as she steered him to her entrance. Then he sank inside her in one fluid motion and she immediately cried out, her nails digging into his shoulders. He chewed on his lower lip as he eased in and out of her, trying hard to stave off the sparkling feeling that twisted in his lower abdomen.

'Ethan.' Her face flushed as the movement of her hips synchronised with his motions. 'That feels so good.'

They were in complete agreement on that one. She was tight and slick, and he seemed to harden further, knowing that he was the reason for her body's reaction. He gritted his teeth, opened her legs wider, deepened his thrusts.

'Don't stop.' She punctuated her words with brief, distracted kisses. 'Don't stop ... Don't stop ...'

Her commands rushed straight to his groin, and a flood of disjointed sexual thoughts flashed through his mind, signalling the beginning of the end. He quickened his thrusts, positioning himself so the base of his cock made maximum contact with her clit. She arched into him, pressing her nearly nude form against his fully clothed one, and mumbled a stream of breathy incoherencies before her body went rigid and she released a strangled cry. Ethan was in awe; having her come apart like that in his arms had suddenly topped his unspoken list of his most rewarding experiences. The feeling of her contracting around him caused the sparkling sensation in his abdomen to explode at long last, and he collapsed on top of her with a shudder.

They were silent for a while, clinging to each other as their heartbeats returned to normal. Then Ethan let out a sigh he hadn't realised he'd been holding and spoke first, his voice rusty. 'Dear *Penthouse* …'

Rei burst out laughing.

'Something unexpected happened today in my studio,' he continued.

She cocked an eyebrow. 'Unexpected?'

'That's right, you had this all planned out.'

'Not really. I couldn't predict how you were going to act. For a moment, I thought it really wasn't going to happen. All I could do was cross my fingers and hope for the best.'

'I commend you on your efforts.'

Rei let out a gusty laugh. 'Thanks to those efforts, I

think it's safe to say that our friendship has been effectively ruined.'

He brushed his lips over hers. 'Whatever. We'll make new friends.'

'Fair enough.' She slipped her fingers inside the back pockets of his jeans. 'Maybe next time we can do this without your clothes on, and you can try your hand at seducing *me*, cowboy.'

'I think that can be arranged.'

She rolled out from beneath him and reached for her corset as if to dress, but he grabbed her wrist and pulled her back to him. 'Now that I think about it, I don't know how I feel about other people seeing the photos we took today,' he murmured. 'What exactly are you planning on being famous for again?'

She grinned as she gave him a tap on his nose with her fingertip. 'Getting exactly what I want.'

The Boy Across the Hall
Kathleen Tudor

Kaylee shifted the grocery bags on her hips and started up the second flight of stairs. Her frown turned to a smile, however, when she saw Arthur coming down from the third-floor landing with some sort of messenger bag slung over his shoulder. 'Arthur!' she exclaimed, pleased as always to see him. He was sexy in a geeky sort of way, always blushing or stammering when he saw her, but she didn't mind. She loved the way his freckles made him look boyish, and the way his brown hair always looked like he'd just run his hands through it. And she loved those sexy green eyes that he hid behind his glasses.

'Oh, uh, good afternoon, Kaylee,' he said, sliding to one side as if to put as much distance between them as possible. At first she'd thought he hated her, but she was starting to realise that he was just painfully shy.

'Help me carry my groceries?' she asked, cocking one

hip at him in an invitation to take the bag balanced there. He looked startled, as if he knew he should have offered and was surprised that he hadn't done so, and reached for the bag. He almost spilled it in his haste, but Kaylee held it steady until he took it from her, and then shifted her other bag to the centre and continued up the stairs with Arthur trailing after.

He waited patiently as she unlocked her door, then followed her inside. Kaylee set her bag down and started to put things away. 'Would you like something to drink?' she asked, smiling at him. Arthur was still standing awkwardly just inside the doorway holding her second bag.

'Um, no, I'd better be going. Thank you.' He stepped forward quickly and set the bag down on the counter beside the first one, then nodded to her and practically fled.

Kaylee sighed as she crossed the room to shut the door behind him. She'd tried being friendly and patient, but Arthur was sort of lost in his own world and oblivious to her interest. And she *was* interested. There was something about him that warmed her, and in those rare moments when he forgot to be nervous and actually interacted with her, it seemed like he was interested, too.

So how to get him out of his shell ...

* * *

Arthur could have kicked himself as he went down the apartment building stairs, but he waited until he got outside to swear softly about it. Kaylee was smart, gorgeous and had the best smile, which she freely offered to him whenever they ran into one another. He'd had a crush on her since she first moved in several months before, and he'd been trying to work up the courage to ask her out practically ever since.

He sighed and adjusted his satchel as he walked the half-block to the deli where he'd planned to spend the afternoon. He'd thought Kaylee was just being polite, but in retrospect maybe she'd wanted to hang out with him. He should have said yes, and left only if things got awkward. Then he sighed in resignation. More awkward, he admitted to himself.

He sat down with his sandwich and pulled out his tablet. He was planning to spend most of this afternoon playing with a couple of logo designs for a client and working up sketches for a third. As he toyed with the designs, his mind wandered back to Kaylee. She'd looked so sweet and inviting, standing there with ice-cream in her hands and a smile on her face, that all he'd been able to think about was how soft her lips would be, or how small and warm she would feel if he stepped forward and pulled her into his arms.

He'd never really been bold, but he knew his confidence had been even lower since his last girlfriend. She hadn't just broken his heart, she'd eviscerated him, and he was having a hard time bouncing back. Somehow he was going to have to figure out how to get past that hurdle, though. A gorgeous girl like Kaylee wasn't going to stay single for long in this city, and the last thing he wanted was to watch her walk up the stairs with some other guy.

When he got home in the early evening, he found a piece of paper just inside his door. He unfolded it to find a home-printed invitation. Classy, he thought, sort of cookie-cutter, but understated and the colours are good.

The invitation stated that he was invited to a party at the home of Kaylee Thomas to celebrate 'The Joy of Living – Come Play with Me!' at 7 p.m. that Friday. She'd filled in all of her information, and he wondered if he'd been a last-minute afterthought because he'd run into her, or if she'd planned to invite him all along. He considered saying no, just to avoid offending her, but of the two options – 'Yes, I'll be there' or 'No, count me out' – she'd checked the 'yes' option with a large, sparkly purple mark.

He drew a smiley face next to her mark with a handy green pen, then stepped out into the hall and slid the invitation under her door. *OK, Kaylee, you got me.*

He would put a move on her at the party. But no, that was too obvious, and there might be too many strangers there – and too many of her friends getting between them. He bit his lip as he shut his apartment door and leaned back against it. There had to be a way to ask her out at the party without seeming like a jerk.

When he realised what he had to do, it struck him as so obvious that he was shocked it hadn't occurred to him before.

* * *

Kaylee had dinner set to go and the house cleaned by early afternoon on Friday. She'd taken the day off because she knew she'd be too excited to work, and, sure enough, her nerves were dancing as she waited for the hours to tick by. She was scrubbing the counters for the second time when a knock at her door startled her so badly that she jumped and dropped her sponge.

She glanced quickly at the kitchen clock, but it was only 6.30. Could a salesman have got into their building? She picked up the sponge and tossed it in the sink, stripped off her rubber gloves and went to check the peephole, where she was surprised to see Arthur standing and looking especially handsome in a button-down shirt.

As soon as she opened the door he whisked a bouquet of flowers from behind his back, and Kaylee couldn't help giving a girly purr of appreciation as she took them. She buried her face in the fragrant blooms, inhaling deeply as she enjoyed the scents of lilies and carnations. When she looked up again, Arthur laughed.

'You have pollen all over your nose,' he said, and reached up unselfconsciously to brush it away from her nose and cheeks. She froze, holding perfectly still as if to move would be to scare him away.

'You're early,' she finally said, smiling at him to show that she didn't mind.

'Oh! I wanted to bring the flowers over and ask if you needed any help, you know, getting things ready.' He shuffled his feet, and Kaylee stepped out of the doorway and gestured him in before answering.

When the door was safely shut behind her, Kaylee leaned against it and smiled. 'Well, I have been getting things ready all day, so I think I'm pretty much set. But now that everyone's here, we can get the party started early.'

Arthur looked worried as he looked around the apartment. 'People are already here? I thought half an hour would be early enough! I wanted to ask you out before anyone else showed up.' All of a sudden he seemed to realise what he had said, and his face went slowly red as he turned to stare at her.

Kaylee laughed, delighted, and went to find a vase for her flowers. 'You did?'

'Well, yeah.' He paused, then added, 'I've had a crush on you since you moved in here, but I never really knew what to say to you.' He looked around again, then followed her into the little kitchen area.

'That would have been a good place to start,' she pointed out. She trimmed the stems and arranged the flowers, cheered and delighted by the bright colours. 'Lilies are my favourites, by the way. Thank you.'

'I'll remember. I thought you said everyone was here. Where are they?' He looked around the small one-bedroom as if he were afraid that a dozen people were going to pop out of the closet.

'I got sick of waiting for you to work up the courage, so I decided to send a little invitation of my own. You *are* the party, Arthur.' She moved out of the tiny kitchen and shrugged, suddenly nervous. 'If you want to be.'

Arthur laughed and stepped closer, and suddenly those sexy green eyes were smouldering. He touched the tip of his nose to hers, their eyes locked, and then he slowly tipped his head and brought his mouth to hers.

Kaylee relaxed into the kiss, letting the warmth of it flow over her from head to toe, warming something inside that she hadn't even realised was in need of warming. When he turned the heat up, taking the kiss from a sweet simmer to something deliciously spicy, Kaylee followed his lead, nipping at his lower lip to encourage the aggressive move.

When they pulled apart again, both of them were breathing heavily. 'I have fish ready to bake,' she said. 'And wine. I have wine, if you'd like some.'

'Wine would be good,' Arthur said, and the way he

moved was no longer nervous and shy but confident and even slightly suggestive. Kaylee stepped back into the kitchen to pour them each a glass of chardonnay, and he took his and clinked it lightly against hers. The little ring of the glasses touching seemed to resonate up and down her spine, and she shivered happily as she led the way to her couch.

When he sat down a foot away from her, Kaylee scooted closer, and Arthur set his glass down on the coffee table, untouched. He put an arm around her and she felt herself warmed from the inside as if she were half-drunk, though her wine glass was just as full as his was. She set it beside his – she actually preferred cider anyway – pulled both of her feet up under her and snuggled into him.

'I feel like a teenager again,' he joked, and Kaylee snorted, remembering her own slightly wild teen years.

'Not me. When I was a teenager, I would have been sprawled on the couch making out,' she teased. She was afraid of scaring him off with the details, but he didn't look scared. In fact, he grinned at her as he took his glasses off and set them beside the wine. Then he leaned towards her, moving his body over hers slowly, easing her onto the couch.

'Like this?' he asked, covering his body with hers at last. She shivered again, pressing up into him to feel the full weight of his body against hers. 'Or more like this?'

He kissed her, his tongue seeking and gaining entrance as he teased at her mouth. 'Or maybe this?' This time his kiss came down on her neck, nibbling at her throat and nipping along the line of her jaw, teasing with the tip of his tongue. She moaned as she tipped her head back to enjoy the sensations, but something was missing.

'You forgot a little bit of this,' she said. She grabbed his hand and pulled it up to her breasts, and this time it was his turn to moan. She dug her hands into that shaggy hair as he continued to explore every contour of her neck, and she whimpered happily as he shifted and pressed his erection against her. Her sounds of pleasure seemed to encourage him, and she arched up into his hands as he fondled her breasts and pinched her nipples.

'Where were you when I was in high school?' he asked, his breath hot on her ear as he leaned in close. She sighed, melting happily into the sensation.

'I take it you're not hungry?'

Arthur bit down on her earlobe, sending chills through her. 'On the contrary,' he whispered, 'I'm starving. Just maybe not so much for fish right now.'

Kaylee felt the perverse urge to tease him, despite the difficulty she'd gone to to get him here and the pleasure she was enjoying in his presence. 'What are you hungry for?' she asked as innocently as possible.

Arthur laughed and sat up, and she was afraid for a moment that she *had* startled him away. He lifted a hand to her face and traced a finger over her eyebrow, down her hairline, across her cheek, and over her lips. Kaylee held as still as possible, her eyes falling closed as she followed his finger with her awareness. He left a tingling wake across her face and a craving for more.

'I've been hungry to touch you and to taste you for months now, and I've been starving myself out of politeness,' he said, smiling. His hand cupped her cheek for a second, then drifted lower to cup her breasts instead.

'Politeness is overrated,' Kaylee said.

'You know, I think you might be right.' He grabbed the hem of her shirt, and – despite what they'd just agreed about politeness – waited until she nodded before drawing it up and off of her. Her skin was sensitised and eager, and she could almost feel the air moving against it as she waited for his touch. She reached back to unfasten her bra, unwilling to wait for the polite moment. When she tossed it away, Arthur's eyes fastened on her breasts and he groaned.

She reached down to cup his erection, and he ground against her hand before easing back and lowering himself to taste her breasts. She was ready for everything, but he moved slowly, licking her skin and tasting her as he moved over the top of one breast and down under the other, kissing or nibbling at the flesh as he went. By the time his mouth found her nipple and drew it into her mouth, she was ready to scream for mercy.

Kaylee had never come just from nipple stimulation before, but she had heard that some women could, and right now she was ready to believe it. She gasped in pleasure and grabbed him by the hair, this time holding him against her. He chuckled as he continued to suckle and tease, and the vibrations shot through her like an electrical charge. 'Oh, God,' she whimpered, and her sounds only made him chuckle again and start it all over. When he switched to the other breast, Kaylee decided that she was going to die of sheer frustrated arousal.

The more she moaned and bucked and wiggled beneath him, the more Arthur seemed to enjoy sucking, nipping, licking and teasing her nipples. He hummed happily, and she finally had to push him away, sure that her spine was going to explode from electrical overload.

She wiggled out from underneath him, then knelt in front of him, teasing at the waistband of his trousers. 'You going to let me have a turn?' she asked coyly.

Arthur's blush returned, much to her pleasure. 'You do that and the fun will all be over before it even gets started,' he said.

'Nonsense. There's lots of ways to have fun,' she murmured, and he didn't protest as she undid his trousers and slid them off. His cock was bigger than she'd expected, and it swayed slightly with the rhythm of his pulse, eager for her.

Kaylee leaned in close, letting her breath tease over

his shaft, torturing him with her nearness for a moment before allowing her tongue to dart out and sample his smooth skin. He groaned and dropped his head back as she teased him with her tongue, giving short, light licks without giving him what he really wanted.

'Kaylee,' he moaned, and the way he groaned her name made her realise for the first time that he'd probably fantasised about this moment a hundred times. It was incredibly erotic, but for a second she was almost crushed by the weight of the pressure. What if she wasn't as good as he'd imagined?

She licked her way delicately to his tip, then circled the crown with her tongue before sucking the head of his cock into her mouth and holding it there against the length of her tongue. He moaned and bucked his hips up, but kept his hands to himself, letting her control the pace. She liked that.

'You're delicious,' she said, teasing him for another moment before she finally let his cock slide all the way past her lips and deep into her mouth. He groaned again as she swallowed around him, and suddenly the sounds he was making were too much to resist. Even as she started to bob up and down on his cock, she reached into her own pants and began to stroke her wet slit.

When Arthur noticed what she was doing with her free hand, he hissed through his teeth and squeezed his eyes shut, his hands balling into fists and his cock twitching.

Then he opened his eyes and stared at her with an intensity like the sun, and she moaned as she felt the weight of his attention and arousal.

His eyes widened a fraction, then his cock pulsed and she tasted the hot, salty semen as it spilled into her mouth. Her fingers worked frantically on her clit and she shuddered hard as she swallowed him, the sound of his shouts of pleasure giving her the last tiny push that she needed to join him in pleasure. She moaned loudly as she came, finally letting his cock slip away from her mouth to throw her head back and embrace the pleasure.

It shot through her, coursing up and down her spine and pooling in her fingers and toes with sharp tingles. She panted as she sat back and looked up at him.

His eyes were fixed on her. 'That was incredible. You're so beautiful, Kaylee.' He reached out, cupped her cheeks with both hands and drew her forward. She leaned into him, passing the taste of his come back to him and drinking in the taste of his mouth. Her spine felt rubbery with the aftereffects of pleasure, but she'd worked to get him here and she wasn't ready to be done with him yet.

Kaylee pulled Arthur's shirt off and straddled his lap, sinking deeply into a kiss that slowly warmed from deeply and quietly erotic to something hot and spicy and immediate. They both made quiet, aroused noises, and she smiled into the kiss when she felt life throbbing into his cock once again.

'Come to my bedroom, Arthur,' she whispered. 'Let's play.'

He stood, took her hand and followed her as if he were in some sort of aroused daze, and Kaylee felt like she was walking on air. Her body still stirred with desire for him as she moved to the bedroom and dug into a drawer. He looked surprised at what she pulled out.

'Is it safe?' he asked, holding the glass dildo up to the light.

Kaylee smiled. 'It's made of the same stuff as Pyrex. It won't break. Come on, it feels incredible. Come play with me.' She danced backward towards the bed and lay down. She shimmied out of her pants and tossed them aside. When she opened her legs for him, he knelt between them, confused.

'I've never done this,' he admitted.

'Just fuck me with it. It's OK,' she said, and he hesitantly touched the cold glass tip to her clit. She let out a little mew of pleasure at the cold of the glass against her steaming sex, and he pressed a little harder, sliding it along her pussy lips with a firm pressure until he found her hole. Kaylee planted her feet and lifted her hips, begging him with her body language to spear her on the beautiful glass cock.

Arthur pushed, and the thick bulb of the head slid inside her, filling her with its solid, weighty presence. When it was as deep as it could go, he started to slide it slowly out again.

142

'Enough teasing. Fuck me with it! Please, Arthur!'

And he did. She stifled a scream of pure pleasure as the glass cock plunged back into her and he fucked her hard. There was something different and exciting about the glass, not just because it was cold at first, but because even the hardest cock was flesh – yielding. The glass was hard and solid and it was her body that had to yield, conforming to the shape and weight of the dildo without compromise.

The stimulation was intense and incredible, and she was so close that she could taste the orgasm. 'Touch my clit,' she said, almost weeping from the thorough and incredible fuck he was giving her. He waited for her to look at him – to meet his eyes – before he reached for her clit.

The first touch gave her what she needed, and she lost his eyes as she bucked, out of control as if an electrical current were running through her entire body. She screamed with the intensity of it, trying to bury her pleasure in her pillow so the neighbours wouldn't complain. Again.

Arthur had left the glass inside her when she came, and the feelings of clamping around that firm surface only intensified the pleasure. When she looked up at him, he was stroking his erection, his eyes roving along her body.

'Have you ever tried anal sex?' she asked, still trying to catch her breath. Arthur looked panicked, and she laughed. 'It's OK. Maybe another time.' She pulled the dildo out of her pussy and met his eyes as she licked her cream off of the warmed glass. He groaned as he watched her. 'Condoms in the drawer.'

Arthur grabbed one and she took it from him and rolled it on over the satiny smoothness of his erection. She was about to ask him if he wanted her in another position, but he moved on top of her in the blink of an eye, recaptured her lips and kissed her with an intensity that made her twitch her hips towards him.

'I want to make you scream like that again,' he growled. He thrust forward, burying himself inside of her, and she gasped and lifted her legs to wrap them around his waist.

'Sounds like a good foundation for a relationship,' she gasped, and then all words were gone as he started to fuck her. Arthur might not have been as firm as glass, but he was larger than the dildo and she was already incredibly sensitive from the foreplay and two orgasms. She trembled with the force of her arousal as she rose up to meet his thrusts, her breath coming in short gasps.

His own breath was fast and ragged, and she held back, knowing that he would come with her and wanting this to last. His cock slammed into her again and again, and she danced on the edge of orgasm through sheer force of will, her entire body clenching with the need for release.

When she finally lost the battle, they bucked together,

burying their faces in each other's necks to drown out the sounds of their passion. They collapsed in a sweaty tangle, smiling and chuckling at one another, and Kaylee felt the warmth of contentment settle over her as she snuggled up to him.

'So, would you like to go out with me some time?' Arthur asked into her hair.

Kaylee laughed. 'Don't you think it would be more fun to stay in?'

Unfinished Business
Elenya Lewis

The temperature must have been nearly 35 degrees. The late-afternoon air was thick with hair spray and sweaty bodies, closely packed and gyrating to music too loud to be readily discernible. The bass was so heavy Adam could feel the chains on his trousers humming, even though he was standing still. He was attempting to look nonchalant as he leaned on the long outdoor bar, but he was anything but casual. He was watching like a hawk.

Hannah. He had not seen Hannah once in the eight years since they had left high school. Until the couple of emails they had exchanged in the last few months, he had not spoken to her since they broke up for the last time in sixth form. She had been pretty back then, but now she was a sight for sore eyes. He couldn't tear his gaze away. She was dancing as though the rest of the world did not exist and yet, Adam imagined, she knew exactly what effect she was having on those around her. She was everything he remembered and so much more. The tight latex shirt and electric-blue miniskirt accentuated that her body was that of a young woman now, not an awkward 17-year-old. His cock hardened every time he looked at her, and he was thankful for the loose-fitting black trousers that allowed him to maintain some shred of dignity. When he thought of how he'd wanted her back then he almost laughed; it was nothing compared to how he ached for her now.

She'd glanced at him a couple of times. He was exactly where she'd asked him to be but she hadn't come over to speak to him yet. Her eyes raked over him now and then with a sly satisfaction, teasing him, tempting him. He wondered what she wanted. She had emailed to say that they had 'unfinished business' and that she needed to see him. She would not explain what she had in mind, and they had exchanged little more by way of greeting or catching up. Adam had thought a lot about what 'unfinished business' might mean, and his imagination had conjured up one or more possibilities, but he had been slightly nervous when they had set a time and a date to meet, at this bar at a festival they had been to once as teenagers.

Over the years that had passed, Adam had often found his thoughts straying to Hannah. His biggest regret was that they had never had sex during their time together.

There was no doubt that she'd adored him, but she had been sex-shy and ultimately her fear of letting him down had driven them apart. He had waited for her. He'd had other relationships since, sure, and he'd fucked enough women that he'd stopped keeping count, but, if he was honest, he had been saving some part of himself for Hannah all this time. She turned towards him with a twist of her hips, and his cock twitched. Even now, his desire for her lay within him like a cat, pretending to be lazy and relaxed, but rearing up at even the tiniest movement.

She stalked towards him like a lioness eyeing its prey. She really *was* different now. She would never have swaggered like that when he knew her. With a stab of worry, he wondered if she'd still be all the things he'd loved about her so long ago. She glanced at him and leaned over the bar, motioning towards the bartender, giving him a delicious view of her ass, still round and perfect. Hannah would always be slightly plump, but she wore it in all the right places. Large plastic beaker of water in hand, she turned to him and drank greedily, her face a picture of satisfaction at the cool liquid. Adam tried not to look dumbfounded, but honestly he was blown away. He could not have imagined that the teenage object of his affection could be standing in front of him so attired, so confident, so sexy. He was speechless with lust, imagining only peeling off the layers of her clothing one by one in order to touch her, to lick her nipples, to tease her until she dripped with desire, and then fuck her until he screamed her name in spasms of ecstasy.

She said something, but Adam couldn't hear a thing. He shrugged and pointed at his ears. She leaned in and yelled.

'Hi!' Her breath tickled his neck and the proximity of her blooming skin sent shivers down his spine. She was radiating heat. He desperately tried to pull together his wayward thoughts.

By way of a reply, he smiled at her and she smiled back. She was wearing dramatic black eye-liner and her grey eyes were pools in her face, deep and clear. Christ, she was gorgeous. Adam cursed himself that he hadn't appreciated her more. He leaned in and yelled back: 'How have you been, Hannah?'

She studied his face, apparently thinking over his words. She motioned towards the exit from the field and leaned in again. He instinctively tried to lean back a bit – it wouldn't do for her to realise how hard he was for her.

'Shall we go somewhere?' she yelled. Adam couldn't gauge from her tone what she wanted. He wondered again what the 'unfinished business' might be. He swallowed and nodded. Where was his quiet calm now?

They didn't try to speak as they pushed their way through bodies to get to the gate. Once or twice he lost sight of her, only for her to reappear like a bolt of lightning with a flash of blue or a swish of hair. His mouth was dry. It had been so long since he'd seen her last. She had filled out, and grown up, and he wanted to fuck her. If he were to guess at their unfinished business, it would be this. He had thought of little else, but had not considered that perhaps she had a boyfriend – or a girlfriend – or simply did not want to fuck him. His palms were slightly sweaty and he hoped he wasn't going to make an idiot of himself.

At length, they made it out to the almost empty refreshment area, strewn with cups and napkins and a couple of people having quiet conversations. Behind them, the thud of the dancefloor mercifully became a background noise, no longer so loud that Adam couldn't think straight. Hannah pulled him towards an empty table. They sat in hard plastic chairs and looked at each other. Hannah studied his face with half a smile. Adam resisted the urge to grin. She was still so cute, and yet so unbelievably sexy. A perfect balance of girl and woman. He wanted to capture the moment and keep it for ever.

'How have you been, Hannah?' Adam asked finally. Hannah blinked slowly, as though she had been far away.

'I ...' she began, but trailed off, apparently unsure what to say. She took a deep breath. 'Adam ... I never stopped thinking about you.' She looked away, all her cocky sex appeal gone, no longer a woman but the same vulnerable girl he remembered. Adam thought back to the day they had split up, and how he had just felt numb watching her run away, tears in her eyes.

'Hannah,' he said gently. He didn't know what else to say.

'I asked you here,' said Hannah slowly, not daring to look at him, 'because I've been thinking something for a while, and I need to get it off my chest.' Adam's heartbeat sped up. Could it be? His cock ached as he thought about how much he wanted her, how much it would mean to him to make love to her like it was their first time and the years between them hadn't really passed.

'What do you mean?' he asked. 'What unfinished business have we got?' he added, in case she was talking about something else. Taking another deep breath, Hannah looked into his eyes.

'I want to have sex with you,' she said quietly. Adam could barely believe his ears.

'Pardon?' he said, wanting to be sure.

'I want you to fuck me,' Hannah said. She didn't pause before saying it. There was no fear or hesitation in her voice.

Adam was once again speechless. His mind reeled for a few moments, but he had been waiting for those words for years. His surprise was mostly that he'd heard them for real, and not in some masturbatory fantasy. He got up from his chair, pulled Hannah out of hers and wrapped his arms around her, pleased that he could still fit her snugly in against his body. He kissed her with a ferocity that had spent eight years and then some brewing, hungry lips crushed against her, his tongue dipping into her mouth, savouring her once again, foreshadowing all that he needed to do to her. He pulled away quickly, leaving Hannah gasping for breath.

'Christ, Hannah,' he said, panting, 'I've waited my whole life to hear you say that.'

The next fifteen minutes were a complete blur. Neither said anything as they made their way to Adam's tent. They took their time over the journey, stopping to kiss and to look at each other and to bite lips and imagine what they were about to do. Hannah's eyes were alight with lust, her every movement a seduction, an invitation. Adam was speechless at his need to remove her clothing, to caress her naked form and touch her most intimate places. It was an act of love, not merely sex, he realised. They had waited too long for this to be just a simple fuck.

They reached Adam's tent. Adam went for the zip but Hannah pulled him away.

'No,' she said, 'I want to do it out here.'

Adam gasped.

'In the open?' he asked, slightly incredulous.

'Yes,' she said, pulling him towards the grass between the tents.

'Wait,' said Adam, dipping into his tent to find a

condom. He came back a moment later. 'OK.' He allowed Hannah to tug him by the hand until she found a spot she thought was worthy. The sun was setting, and the tents were beginning to go dim around them, the sky awash with hues of orange and red. The air was warm and quiet, almost pensive. Adam was struggling to contain himself. Hannah sat down on the grass, leaned back onto her elbows and spread her legs invitingly.

He knelt down in front of her, trailed fingers slowly up her bare legs towards the hem of her skirt, watching her expression change from mocking to slightly breathless. Smiling, he climbed on top of her, pressing his cock against the fabric of her skirt. She lay down on the ground and he leaned in to kiss her. 'We've been here before,' he murmured into her cheek, his breath hot against her skin.

'You weren't doing this though,' she murmured back, guiding his hand towards her breast, firm under the shiny shirt. He squeezed gently, somehow worried that she was about to tell him off. Hannah chuckled. 'You remember that time John Millington tried to grope me and you hit him for me?' she said.

Adam chuckled back but he was distracted by the pearling nipple appearing underneath the latex. He squeezed harder, the feel of flesh in his hand turning him on even more. He stifled a moan by kissing Hannah again, his tongue probing through her gasp-parted lips. He wanted to touch her pussy, to hear her moan for him, but he wanted to take things slow. Although struggling to contain his lust, somehow he knew this had to be special, done properly. He sat up so that he could touch her other breast, studying the soft peaks underneath his hands, enjoying the pleasure on Hannah's face at his reaction to her.

'I want this off,' he said, tracing a finger underneath the top to tickle the skin beneath. Hannah licked her lips.

'There's a zip at the back,' she said. Adam climbed off and pulled Hannah over onto her front. She landed with a soft *oof*, her skirt riding up her ass in a way that Adam found irresistibly sexy. He fumbled at the zip a little with shaking fingers but managed to undo it. Slowly he peeled the shirt away from her skin, then, before she could get up, he pulled her skirt up and plunged his hand down the back of her pants, fondling her soft cheeks and slowly running his finger between them, down towards the warmth of her pussy. Hannah moaned and arched her back and Adam used his other arm to pin her to the floor. She moaned again and bashed her fists against the ground.

'Something wrong?' asked Adam, amused at the power of his position.

'Touch me,' hissed Hannah, laying her head on the ground in submission. She was grinding her ass against his hand, trying to inch his finger towards her, trying to get him to touch her. He laughed and pulled a little further away. Hannah let out a strangled half-sob. With his spare hand, Adam grabbed hold of her hair and pulled her head off the ground slightly so he could whisper in her ear.

'Like this?' he said, before reaching down into her pants, dragging his finger across her delicious hole again before dipping just inside her sodden pussy. Hannah sighed appreciatively.

Adam pushed his finger in a little bit further.

'Christ, you're wet,' he moaned into her hair.

'Uh huh,' was Hannah's muffled response.

It took all Adam's willpower not to pull down his own pants and fuck her right there. Not yet, he thought. Hannah moaned again as he pulled his hand out of her pants.

'Please,' she whispered.

'Not yet,' he replied softly, and rolled her over onto her back again. She gazed up at him, her eyes drowning pools of silver, her lips rounded and full. Adam had a stab of nostalgia and gently pulled her face in to kiss her. 'I've missed you,' he said, his voice barely audible.

Hannah leaned her forehead against his.

'Me too,' she said.

Adam's aching cock would not allow him to get totally lost in the romance of the moment, however much the rest of him wanted to, and he peeled the rest of Hannah's top away from her damp skin. He marvelled at her breasts, which he had long wanted to see naked.

155

'I wanted to kick John Millington's head in for touching you before me,' he said with half a smile.

'You always were too protective of me,' said Hannah. She bit her lip. 'I'm not a girl any more,' she said with a hint of defiance, tracing a finger lightly around the curve of her breast in a way which made Adam's breath catch in his throat.

'No, you're not,' Adam said absently, his eyes still on Hannah's beautiful cleavage, pale white with pink nipples, hard and demanding. He took one in his mouth, flicking the taut nipple over and over with his tongue, mirroring the movement on her other breast with his finger, the rest of the flesh cupped in his hand. Hannah whined, her breath quickening. She was beginning to tremble and Adam could see her elbows quaking as she tried to hold herself up. He dragged his attention away from her bosom to lay her down again. Running his fingers through her hair, he smiled at her breathy, aroused expression and glazed-over eyes. He needed to touch that beautiful pussy again. He rubbed her breasts with his free hand and traced a finger down the centre of her stomach, following the hollow of her belly as she inhaled sharply and dipping into her shallow navel before stopping just above the waistband of her skirt.

She laid a hand gently on his.

'No fair,' she said, her breathing ragged, 'I want to see skin too.'

'My bad,' replied Adam, grinning. Hannah sat up, splaying her legs out as she did so that he could see her pants and imagine her soft, sweet sex beneath them. His mouth watered as he thought about probing her with his tongue. She took hold of his chin and drew his gaze to her eye level.

'I remember that look in your eyes,' she said quietly, her eyes vulnerable and hurting, 'and it used to scare me. I couldn't understand how you could want me so much. I didn't want to disappoint you.'

She was kneeling in front of him now, and Adam reached around her with both arms and groped her ass, pulling her into him and kissing her, his mind rendered useless at the combination of proximity and flesh and lust. He fumbled for words.

'What do you think now?' he asked, showering her cheeks with kisses as her fingers fidgeted against his lap. He didn't want her to be nervous. He gently kneaded her ass as she thought.

Slowly, her fingers stopped fidgeting and she rested her hands flat against his thighs, before beginning to squeeze. Adam's cock was throbbing against his trousers. Her touch was like an electric current.

'I'm intoxicated by how much you want me,' she whispered into his neck. Her hands started to creep up his thighs towards his crotch and Adam could barely breathe. She let out a low chuckle. 'I'm high on your reaction to me,' she said, biting his neck softly as her hands came to rest on his cock. He moaned.

'I'm all yours,' he said, unable to think about anything but how much he wanted her fingers wrapped around his length. He moaned again, wondering how he was still controlling the insatiable urge to rip his clothes off and fuck her.

Hannah undid the buttons on Adam's shirt one by one, taking her time to press her fingers to his bare skin between each one. She bit her lip as she looked at him, exploring his body with sight as well as touch. Adam was fascinated by the way she drank him in, as though she had never seen a man naked before. As she reached the last button and carefully pulled the shirt off, she met his eyes.

'You really are beautiful, you know that?' she said, her eyes shining. 'I always thought so.'

Adam smiled and rolled his eyes.

'Look at us,' he said, 'like teenagers all over again.'

'I feel like this is my first time,' said Hannah with a smirk.

Adam frowned. 'It isn't, is it?' he asked carefully.

Hannah laughed. 'No', she said. 'But in many ways, you'll always be my first.'

'Something about that just sounds creepy,' said Adam.

'Yeah,' replied Hannah, 'perhaps we should stop talking and just get on with it.'

'I like the talking,' said Adam, removing a hand from Hannah's delightful bottom and kissing her briefly, 'but other things are good too.' His fingers found their way down her pants and back into her delightful wetness and she groaned and kissed him. Her hands were tugging at his belt, deftly sliding the buckle out and pulling at the button of his trousers. Adam could scarcely breathe from the anticipation of her hand on his hard cock. As she slid the zip out of the way and peeled away the waistband of his boxers, they both let out a gasp of arousal.

'Fuck. Me. Now,' hissed Hannah through pursed lips, her hand wrapped around the base of Adam's shaft, groaning with each stroke. Adam nodded breathlessly. The couple pulled apart slowly, discarding their remaining clothing between sneaking peeks at each other's naked body. Whilst not self-conscious as a rule, Adam found himself worrying what Hannah would think of him. He blushed and Hannah giggled.

'You look great,' she said, responding to Adam's unspoken fear.

'So do you,' said Adam, gently touching Hannah's skin. She truly was a wonderful sight with no clothes on, soft wispy hairs covering her mound and her sex glistening with her desire.

'If we do this again,' said Adam, fumbling with the condom packet because he couldn't take his eyes away from Hannah's blushing sex, 'I am going to go down on you.'

Hannah stroked Adam's cock, making it even harder to concentrate on the condom, and she leaned in and kissed him.

'I'd like that,' she whispered.

Condom finally in place, Adam trembled as he positioned himself over Hannah's supine form, resting gently in the grass.

'Are you ready?' he asked. Hannah's eyes were wide, whether with fear or anticipation Adam wasn't sure. She nodded. He slowly guided his cock between her swollen lips. He sucked in a breath, pleasure shooting through him in fiery tendrils. She was hot and tight and everything he had imagined all these years.

'Fuck, you feel good,' he hissed. He slowly drew out and pushed back in again with a small moan. Hannah smiled and arched her hips upwards towards him, to pull him deeper. He leaned down to kiss her, enjoying the feel of her hard nipples pushing into his chest and her soft skin against his own. She looked to be away with the fairies, an easy smile of peace and pleasure all over her face.

'I could do this all night,' she said, gripping his forearms and kissing him back, her tongue exploring him slowly, brushing against teeth and tongue and lips. With a subtle twist of her hips, she took his cock in deeper, eliciting a guttural moan from him. He buried his face in her chest, his breathing laboured and difficult as he resisted the urge to thrust harder. He wanted to take this slow and steady, but the tightness of her sex and the associated satisfaction made it difficult to think. God, he was enjoying this.

Hannah's hand drifted to her clitoris, where she massaged small circles, gasping noisily as she drifted over her sweet spot. The sight of her touching herself tipped Adam's pleasure-addled brain over the edge and he penetrated her deeper, pulling almost all the way out of her before driving back in again, the wet slap of skin against skin almost masked by the animal sounds of pleasure emitted by both of them. With each stroke Hannah moaned, her pitch slowly building and driving Adam wild. The pressure building inside his cock was magnificent. Please, he thought, don't let me come too soon.

He could feel her orgasm building as surely as he could feel his own and, when she gasped, 'I'm almost there,' he nearly came, thinking about how beautiful her climax would be. Then she came, with a scream, spasming and squeezing around Adam's cock. He could hold himself no longer and came a few moments later in an explosive rush of pain and ecstasy and relief. The shuddering aftershocks knocked the breath out of him with their intensity as Hannah's body quivered and jerked underneath him, her hands clutching at him as she moaned. As they both subsided, she began to laugh, and Adam noticed tears at the corners of her eyes.

'What's wrong?' he asked, hoping he hadn't hurt her in his uncontrolled enjoyment. She smiled at him and Adam was reminded of the way she had smiled like that when they had been younger. The startling contrast to the moment they were now sharing hit him like a brick, and he stifled the urge to laugh at the absurdity of what they had just done.

'Nothing,' she said. 'I'm just happy.' She was beginning to relax, her eyes shiny and bright and exhausted all at the same time. Her face was pink and glowing. Adam withdrew and collapsed on the grass next to her, breathing heavily, his arm draped across her chest. They lay there for a few minutes, saying nothing, listening to their frantic heartbeats slowing to a normal pace and enjoying the warmth of their pressed bodies.

At length, Adam realised that they should move or they were liable to fall asleep. He sat up and looked over Hannah's naked form once more, at their clothes lying around in a forgotten heap, and thought about what they'd just done, about what it represented and how long they had waited to do it.

'Would you change anything?' he asked quietly, hoping that Hannah would understand what he meant. She frowned as she considered the question. She smiled softly.

'No,' she whispered, sitting up so that she could wrap her arms around him and plant a kiss on his neck.

She sighed as he pulled her close, and Adam thought

about the years that they had spent together as teenagers, the shy courtship followed by awkward kisses and falling in love and fighting and then eventually going their separate ways. He had often regretted that Hannah had not been the first woman he made love to, but that didn't seem important any more, not compared with the satisfaction and dazzling wonder of the act they had just committed.

'No,' whispered Hannah again, her lips nuzzling Adam's neck, 'that was perfect.'

Try Before You Bi!
Kitt Gerard

'Press down harder on the table top. I want to be able to see where your big creamy tits squashed all over the glass, next time I sit here and eat my dinner!'

Anya's face flushed crimson as she agonised about obeying the demand, and not just because of the wanton, bottom-in-the-air pose it would force her to adopt. Deep down she knew didn't have to do this; she was here by invitation, not command. There was nothing stopping her getting up there and then and walking out the door – except, of course, for the little matter of being completely naked.

She couldn't believe how this was all happening so quickly. Only an hour ago it had just been like any other normal day and now – well!

To be fair, a little part of herself did realise she had largely brought this upon herself. There could be no denying that over the past few weeks at the university sports club she had allowed herself to get into the habit of going into the communal showers just after Tori. That wasn't at all the kind of thing she normally did, but she couldn't seem to help it. Tori had such a fantastic body, she never got tired of secretly looking at her.

To Anya, being involved in the women's football team was just a bit of fun, a way of getting some exercise at the same time as making new friends. But it was obvious it was much more than that to Tori. She was a natural athlete; you could see that from the way she played. She was good enough to earn a place in most guys' teams.

From snatches of conversation she'd eavesdropped on, Anya knew she swam and ran for the uni, as well, and it all showed in her figure. She had a wonderful physique with powerful, square shoulders, lithe, sinuous limbs and a bottom as firm as an unripe peach. She was so toned all over, Anya used to joke to herself that she probably even had muscles in those wonderfully tight-bobbed breasts of hers. After all, there weren't many girls in the changing room whose nips pointed up at the ceiling.

Anya had been confused by her feelings towards Tori right from the first time she'd seen her in the nude and she still didn't understand why she was so dangerously addicted to looking at her. All she knew was that she was like a moth drawn to a flame; she just really got off on drinking in the dark-haired girl's Amazonian curves.

Of course, she'd had to be very careful not to get

caught peeking at her in the showers. Not just by Tori herself, but by any of the other girls. It would have been mortifying if anyone else had picked up on her little deviation. She would never have lived it down if she'd been found out spying on Tori as she uninhibitedly ran her soapy hands all over her bare body.

Especially so if she'd been discovered peering down at Tori's bush – which, she was ashamed to reflect, was all too possible because that was a particular fascination of hers. Tori's pubes were unbelievable, the thickest, most luxuriant sprouting of curls Anya had ever seen down there on anyone. Really, it was just the most amazing tangle of wild growth and Anya had developed all kinds of ruses so she could linger under a nearby showerhead and keep on snatching illicit glimpses of the sporty girl's magnificent black mat.

That, though, was as far as anything had gone – up until now. Then, just after Anya had set off home after practice that evening, she'd spotted Tori trudging along the roadside with her heavy kitbag slung over her shoulder. Of course, she'd stopped straight away to offer a lift and Tori had gladly accepted the ride. It seemed her car was in the garage and she'd been expecting a bus, but it hadn't turned up.

As it happened, her flat wasn't very far away, but they'd chatted animatedly all the way there. It was only after they'd arrived that things had turned upside down when Tori had, seemingly casually, turned towards Anya to ask her if she wanted to come in for a while and then, completely out of blue, leaned over and kissed her full on the lips.

Anya had been shocked – so totally taken by surprise that she'd instinctively recoiled, making it Tori's turn to be confused.

'Hey, I'm sorry. It's just the way you've been eyeing me up at the club every week made me think you were, you know, "into" me. So what's the real situation? Got a boyfriend?'

'Not at the moment – but I've had loads,' Anya had added, a little too hastily.

'It's females only for me, as you might have guessed already. And I have to say, despite the protests, something's still telling me our signals haven't been completely crossed. I still think you're interested in me. Ever been with a girl?'

'No, no, never,' Anya had blustered, colouring up, 'You've got me all wrong.'

'Oh, I really don't think so, babe. Your mouth is saying one thing, but your eyes are definitely saying another. You're a classic bi-curious if ever I met one.'

Anya had had to look away quickly then, afraid her expression would betray her true state of uncertainty. Not that it mattered, because Tori hadn't given up on her hunch just yet.

'Anyway, despite the denials, my invite's still open. The choice is yours, but it seems to me like the perfect chance to find out just how curious you really are. So, why not come on in and have some fun with me?'

Anya's first reaction had been to start up the car and escape but the voice of temptation inside her head had persuaded her that she'd come to uni for new experiences and this certainly counted as that, so ...

So, heart in her mouth, she'd dutifully followed the rangy athlete into her flat and into the unknown.

Straightaway Tori had poured them both a stiff drink, but as she'd thrust the glass into Anya's hand, she'd had a little confession to make.

'I have to own up – I turned down three other offers for lifts before you finally came along.'

'You mean this was planned?' Anya gasped, as the penny dropped.

'Let's just say I thought it was up to me to move things forward – which is why I'm also going to take control now; it'll be better that way. So, for starters, what you're going to do is take off all your clothes whilst I go and get ready. Now don't be coy, it's not as if I've never seen you in the buff before. You're not the only one who's been doing a bit of undercover surveillance in the showers, you know!'

Once Tori had pulled the curtains closed and gone off to the bedroom, though it seemed like madness, Anya hadn't been able to stop herself slowly stripping off until, dizzy with nervous anticipation, she'd perched herself awkwardly on the edge of the sofa without a stitch on.

Her hands had shaken uncontrollably as she gulped down the last of her drink. All the while she'd waited, her mind had raced on, conjuring up vision after vision of the perverted things that might be going to happen to her when Tori got back. She'd still been torn in two, half of her longing to stay and venture into the uncharted world of depravity that Tori was offering, half of her just wanting to grab her clothes and bolt.

Then her mind had been made up for her as Tori returned. No matter what scenarios Anya had been imagining in her head, they had paled to insignificance compared to the reality she'd been presented with now.

Tori was as bare as she was, except, that is, for the extremely sinful device she had belted on round her waist and between her thighs. It was a series of interconnecting leather straps all designed to hold a shield-shaped cup tightly fitted over her entire quim. And standing out of the centre of that triangular plate was the most enormous black rubber dildo.

In response to Anya's sharp intake of breath, Tori had snorted amusedly, 'What were you expecting, pink baby-doll pyjamas? This is my particular thing and, as I reckoned this might possibly be your one and only go at girl-on-girl action, I thought you needed to be shown that it's not all silk camisoles and sixty-nine-ing by soft candlelight. Sometimes it's downright filthy-dirty – as you're about to find out.'

She'd stroked her hand along the thick shaft lovingly. 'I've got a big collection of these beauties, but this is my favourite. There's something about the look of hard black rubber when it's got a gleaming coat of clear lubricant drizzled all over it like this. You'll notice as well that this selection is also an improvement on the original, flesh, male model in that it's ribbed all the way down the shaft with this series of rings. I promise you that when they're going in and out of your pussy, they'll make it purr like it's never done before.'

'I can't possibly –'

'Forget the second thoughts; I'm in charge now. Remember? So, do as I say. Come over here and bend forward over the end of this table.'

Almost as if she'd been mesmerised by the fearsome curve standing out of Tori's flat groin, Anya had swallowed hard and stood up on legs of jelly. Unable to drag her gaze away, she'd made her way over to the steel-and-glass dining table and very, very gingerly laid herself forward over the edge, shuddering as the cold surface touched her berry-hard nipples like she'd been splashed with ice water.

That was how she'd ended up in the situation she was in now: being coarsely urged to sucker her full breasts even harder onto the glass. And the thing was, even though she knew how rudely exposing the pose was going to be, she did, eventually, do as she'd been told. Something about the thought of how erotic she was going to look, presenting herself like that, finally made her accept that this, whatever *this* was, was what she really wanted.

Submitting to desire, she dropped into the truly brazen pose, displaying her private parts fully to Tori, who immediately stepped in close behind her upturned rear to issue new instructions.

'Listen carefully. I want you to move your feet back a little so that you have space to move your arm down and then I want you to put your usual touching fingers on your clit. I want you to bury the tips against your bud and I want you to hold them there as I dock the slippery tip of my big shiny cock into the fold of your sex lips.

'By the way, you needn't bother protesting about that, either, because I know you're ready for it. I saw how wet and swollen you were between your legs when you staggered over to the table just now. So get on with it, but remember, when I press into you, to keep your hand still because I want you to get yourself even more excited thinking what it's going to feel like when I begin to enter you properly. I want you to hold back until you're so turned on, you can't help moving your fingers, can't help masturbating yourself right in front of me.'

171

Anya had to close her eyes tight to shut out the shame before she could obey this latest, incredibly explicit command, but she did do it. Snaking her right arm back and down, she slid her hand up into the fork of her legs to find her clit and the moment she made contact, she felt an escape of viscous fluid drip down her two extended fingers like honey.

She felt very big there, too; much more engorged than usual. A moan escaped her lips at the pleasure of the touch and then straight away it was followed by a deep groan as Tori probed the unyielding fluted end of the dildo forward between her reared-up thighs and pressed it, gently but insistently, into the soft split of her vulva, creaming her backward-facing labia open around it.

As Tori held it there, just as she'd promised, Anya's mind reeled. If it felt so breathtaking just like that, how on earth would it feel when the whole of that monstrous thing was all the way in her?

Her stomach was full of butterflies now. The waiting was torment; she could feel the suspense rising and rising inside. She was glad she was lying down because she was sure, if she had been upright, her legs would have given way completely. And, out of nowhere, a truly coarse picture came into her head of her standing up straight with Tori holding the dildo right on the edge of entering her, just the way it was now, and her fainting away, causing the entire rubber shaft to horn up inside her, all at once. Right to the shield hilt.

And suddenly she was aware that her fingers were rubbing away distractedly at her quim. It was appalling, but just as Tori had wanted, she had got herself so turned on she was actually openly diddling herself in front of her.

She was caught doing it straightaway and immediately felt Tori's hands on her bottom. Cupping a buttock in each palm, Tori began to circle her arms in opposite directions, alternatively pulling Anya's twin cheeks apart and then pressing them closed together. And the way she did it, each time she opened up her bottom crease, it caused her pussy lips to gape wide open and then, when she worked it shut again, it squeezed them deliciously tight together again around the dildo end.

She carried out the manoeuvre maybe half a dozen times just by itself and then the next time, without warning, she inched her hips forward as she opened Anya up and popped the first ring on the dildo inside her elastic-tight labia, making her moan out loud.

All inhibition cast aside now, Anya began to grind her fingers into her throbbing clit, doing it ferociously just so that she could bear the sensation as, relentlessly, Tori's hands began to move together again, slowly piling her intimate flesh up all around the massive rubber intrusion.

When her hands started to move apart again, Anya tried to brace herself ready this time, but still she couldn't keep from making a sound as the second ring was remorselessly eased into her. Once, twice, three times more she had to suffer the shocking introduction of ring shafts before Tori paused to ask, amusedly, 'Do you feel full now?'

'Yes, yes. Really full,' Anya just managed to pant out, no space inside her for breath.

'Well, you should have taken better note when I showed you the dildo before because first of all there's this –' she tugged her hands apart more roughly and to Anya's disbelief worked a sixth ring into her '– and then there's this.' She did it again, forcing ring number seven forward, just managing to cram it in.

Anya was going crazy now, her fingers beating like a whisk.

'I'm going to start moving now,' Tori informed her, dispassionately. 'I want to get you used to it because you need to know that when I finally give you permission to orgasm, I'm going to fuck your brains out with this thing.'

As Tori attempted to withdraw the shaft, Anya's head tipped back, her mouth a silent O of sensual distress as her whole behind spasmed involuntarily as, one by one, each of the rings was pulled out of her. On and on, it quivered until just the tip remained, then Tori made her suffer all over again by slowly inserting the dildo back inside her. Then she did it all over again, and then again, until, before long, she was stroking in and out of Anya steadily.

'Keep touching yourself!' she commanded. 'Keep

rubbing hard as you think what it's going to be like when I finally tell you you can come. Keep going, keep going! But wait until I say!'

'Too late!' Anya suddenly groaned despairingly. 'I can't help it. I'm there already.'

It was true. Completely out of her control, waves of pleasure were pulsing out of her belly now, rippling through her so strongly that she knew that, even if Tori forced her to stop touching herself right there and then, she was still going to climax violently.

Tori laughed wickedly when she learnt of Anya's predicament and straightaway she grabbed hold of the girl's hips and began to ride into her so hard that it nearly lifted her feet off the ground.

Again and again she slapped her muscular hips up against Anya's soft buttocks until her juddering cries made the walls ring. On and on, Tori stroked the dildo rings in and out of her as fast as she could go, making her fanny lips vibrate with such speed, they actually thrummed loudly.

The stimulation was so intense, Anya thought she really was going to pass out. Then, from somewhere far away, she heard a voice bellowing like a beast and realised it was herself, being transported by the most gut-wrenching, body-wracking orgasm she'd ever suffered.

She remained prone on the table for a long time after the fierce come. Partly because her heart was still pounding like a drum from the force of it, but mostly because she was incredibly embarrassed by the amount of noise she knew she'd made and couldn't bear to face Tori.

Eventually, though, she had to move and, levering herself back upright, she turned and braced herself, blushingly, for the comments on her behaviour that were surely due – and she wasn't disappointed.

'Well, well,' Tori quipped, 'thank goodness the neighbours are away. They would have been reporting me for keeping wild animals!'

During the wait, she had been busy removing the dildo strappings from around her middle. Now, though, she paused before unbuckling the final one and, surprisingly, Anya thought she detected a trace of nervousness in Tori's body language, a hint of indecision even.

She was right, too, because Tori had to clear her throat before she could confide quietly. 'Actually, that was very trusting of you – which is why I want to show you the same kind of trust, now. I'm going to share something with you, but you must promise not to spread it about, OK?'

Anya nodded her agreement, though she was completely mystified.

'I don't know whether you twigged,' Tori went on, 'but most weeks I've deliberately displayed myself to you in the showers and afterwards in the changing rooms, just to get you hot. I've seen where your eyes always go, so

I'm sure you've been wondering why I keep my pubic hair like a forest. Well, there is a reason for it and I'm going to show it to you now.'

Saying that, she slipped the final belt free then slowly lifted the dildo base away from her sex and the moment Anya saw behind it, her eyes opened like saucers.

In the enclosed space where the thick rubber shield had been strapped against her skin, Tori's delta was soaked with perspiration and her normally springy mat of pubic hair unnaturally compressed. In truth, it was so wet and flat it was slicked back into a parting, completely revealing the scarlet cleft of her vulva. And there, standing right out from the top of her exposed quim, was the biggest, most incredibly prominent clitoris Anya had ever seen.

'Oh, my God!'

'Now you know why I keep my hair so bushy.' Tori sighed. 'I have to hide this away from general view whenever I'm undressed. So, go on, say it; I know it's what you're thinking. It looks like a little cock, doesn't it?'

Anya couldn't deny it; it did. Tori's actual clit itself resembled nothing more than a smooth crimson helmet that stalked out of her, the size of a tongue tip with the pushed-back, wrinkled collar of its hood surrounding it to form its 'foreskin'.

Tori sat herself down in a nearby armchair, sprawling back deliberately with her legs spread lewdly apart so that Anya could carry on staring with undisguised interest at the engorged mini-erection dangling fatly out of her. Revelling in the attention, she cupped the focus of Anya's lustful gaze gently in her palm and toyed with it loosely for a while before breathing, huskily, 'You know, the second thing people usually say is to ask if they can touch it and, I have to say, I was rather hoping *you* were going to too, as I'm very, very horny now. So, what do you say? Do you want to have a go?'

All Anya could do was nod once, still too shy to openly admit that, at that precise moment, touching Tori's amazing nub was what she wanted to do more than anything else in the world.

'Come on, then,' encouraged the seated girl, beckoning Anya to drop to her knees between her feet. Taking her right hand, she guided it carefully between her thighs and instructed, 'OK, so it may look like a tiny cock, but that's not how you treat it, all right? You don't wank it like a man's penis; it's more like a pinching action. Thumb on one side, forefinger on the other. Yes, that's it. Now, squeeze the hood so it wipes over the swelling, then ease it back again. Ummm, that's good. That's very good.'

Tori's own hands dropped away, leaving Anya working all on her own. She'd been right; it was completely different from masturbating a man. For a start everything was much more slippery, so that the hood of flesh slid back and forth frictionlessly over the oversized cherry of her clit itself. That, in turn, meant there was no way she could ever get a real hold of that sensitive inner tongue. Every time she brought her fingers together, the copiously lubricated protuberance slipped out of grip, retreating and escaping.

However, she must have been doing something right because Tori's eyelids soon started to flutter shut. She began to clench and unclench her fists on the chair arms. Something told Anya to go a little faster, a little harder, now, and when she did Tori ran her fingers through her hair distractedly.

'Oh, yes,' she crooned, 'that's perfect.'

Another minute and Tori was squirming about on the seat, unable to keep still. Again and again, her knees swung shut and gripped Anya's kneeling body tightly as her thighs contracted and relaxed with ever quickening rhythm.

'Just like that,' she half ordered, half begged. 'Keep going just like that.'

It was obvious to Anya that she was taking Tori to orgasm. In fact, she was sure Tori was right on the very edge of coming and all she had to do was be a good girl and keep massaging away just as she'd been told. But just as Tori slowly began to arch back on the chair, straining every one of her ripped muscles towards the moment of release, she realised there was something she really yearned to do.

Unable to resist the urge, she pulled her fingers away at the last moment and buried her head deep between Tori's thighs. In one scoop, she swallowed the whole bulb of Tori's clit into her mouth and began to suck on it like it was a half-eaten lollipop, mercilessly licking the sticky marble of hard flesh with her tongue.

The effect was electric. Tori instantly buckled forward over her, hissing brokenly, 'Oh, you bitch, you bitch, you darling little bitch!' Then the first jolt of climax hit her and her whole body convulsed violently, from head to toe.

Relishing all her newfound power, Anya sucked on Tori remorselessly as she went through her crisis, inflicting terrible anguish on her, wringing wave after wave of jolting ecstasy from her until, at last, she allowed Tori to slump back in the chair, completely spent.

It was only then that she finally released her lips but, as she did so, she couldn't help making a rude slurping noise as the seal broke. Tori was still basking in the sultry afterglow of her climax but nevertheless she sounded unmistakeably pleased with herself at the way her little scheme had worked out, as she fixed Anya with heavy-lidded eyes and murmured, 'Isn't that just the sexiest sound in the whole world? If that doesn't turn you on to going with girls, nothing will.'

'Actually, I'm really not sure,' Anya responded with mock seriousness, enjoying Tori's look of disappointment before hitting her with the punchline.